MANGA MATH MYSTERIES

THE BOOK BANDIT

A Mystery with Geometry

by Melinda Thielbar

illustrated by Candice Chow
and Jenn Manley Lee

#1

GRAPHIC UNIVERSE™ · MINNEAPOLIS · NEW YORK

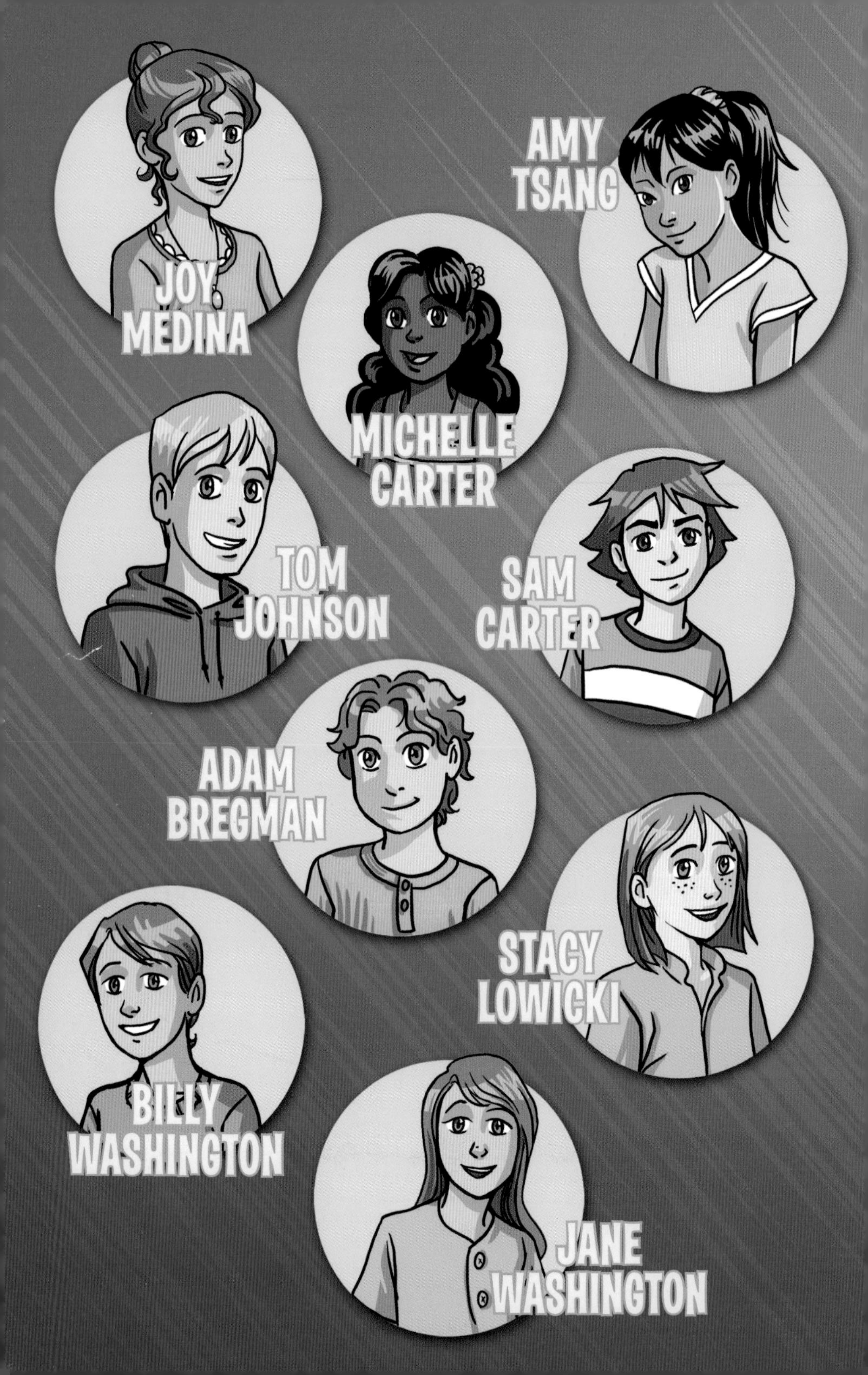
JOY MEDINA
AMY TSANG
MICHELLE CARTER
TOM JOHNSON
SAM CARTER
ADAM BREGMAN
STACY LOWICKI
BILLY WASHINGTON
JANE WASHINGTON

JOY'S MOM

JOY'S DAD

STACY'S MOM

THE LIBRARIAN

What is **geometry**? Geometry is the study and measurement of shapes and their lines, points, and angles. In geometry, you might study two-dimensional (or 2D) shapes like circles, rectangles, and triangles. You might also study three-dimensional (or 3D) shapes like spheres, cubes, and pyramids.

What is **symmetry**? There are different types of symmetry. A figure has symmetry if it can be folded along a line so that the two halves match exactly. When you fold a sheet of paper in half and cut out a heart, the two sides of the heart have mirror symmetry. One side looks like the reflection of the other side in a mirror.

If you turn an object and it still looks the same, it has rotational symmetry. A pizza cut in even slices has rotational symmetry.

An object with translational symmetry looks the same when you move it along a straight line. A train with identical cars has translational symmetry.

J-GN
MANGA MATH
MYSTERIES
399-3766

Story by Melinda Thielbar
Pencils by Candice Chow
Inks by Jenn Manley Lee and Eve Grandt
Coloring by Jenn Manley Lee
Cover coloring by Hi-Fi Design
Lettering by Grace Lu

Graphic Universe™
A division of Lerner Publishing Group, Inc.
241 First Avenue North
Minneapolis, MN 55401 U.S.A.

Website address: www.lernerbooks.com

Library of Congress Cataloging-in-Publication Data

Thielbar, Melinda.
    The book bandit : a mystery with geometry / by Melinda Thielbar ; illustrated by Candice Chow and Jenn Manley Lee.
       p.   cm. — (Manga math mysteries ; #7)
       Summary: When the public library offers a prize for figuring out how a "book monster" sculpture was fit in through a small window in their Reader's Corner, the students of Sifu Faiza's Kung Fu School use geometry to solve the mystery.
       ISBN: 978–0–7613–4909–9 (lib. bdg. : alk. paper)
       1. Graphic novels. [1. Graphic novels. 2. Mystery and detective stories. 3. Geometry—Fiction. 4. Sculpture—Fiction. 5. Libraries—Fiction.] I. Chow, Candice, ill. II. Lee, Jenn Manley, ill. III. Title.
    PZ7.7.T48Boo 2011
    741.5'973—dc22   2010012411

Manufactured in the United States of America
2 –DP – 7/1/11

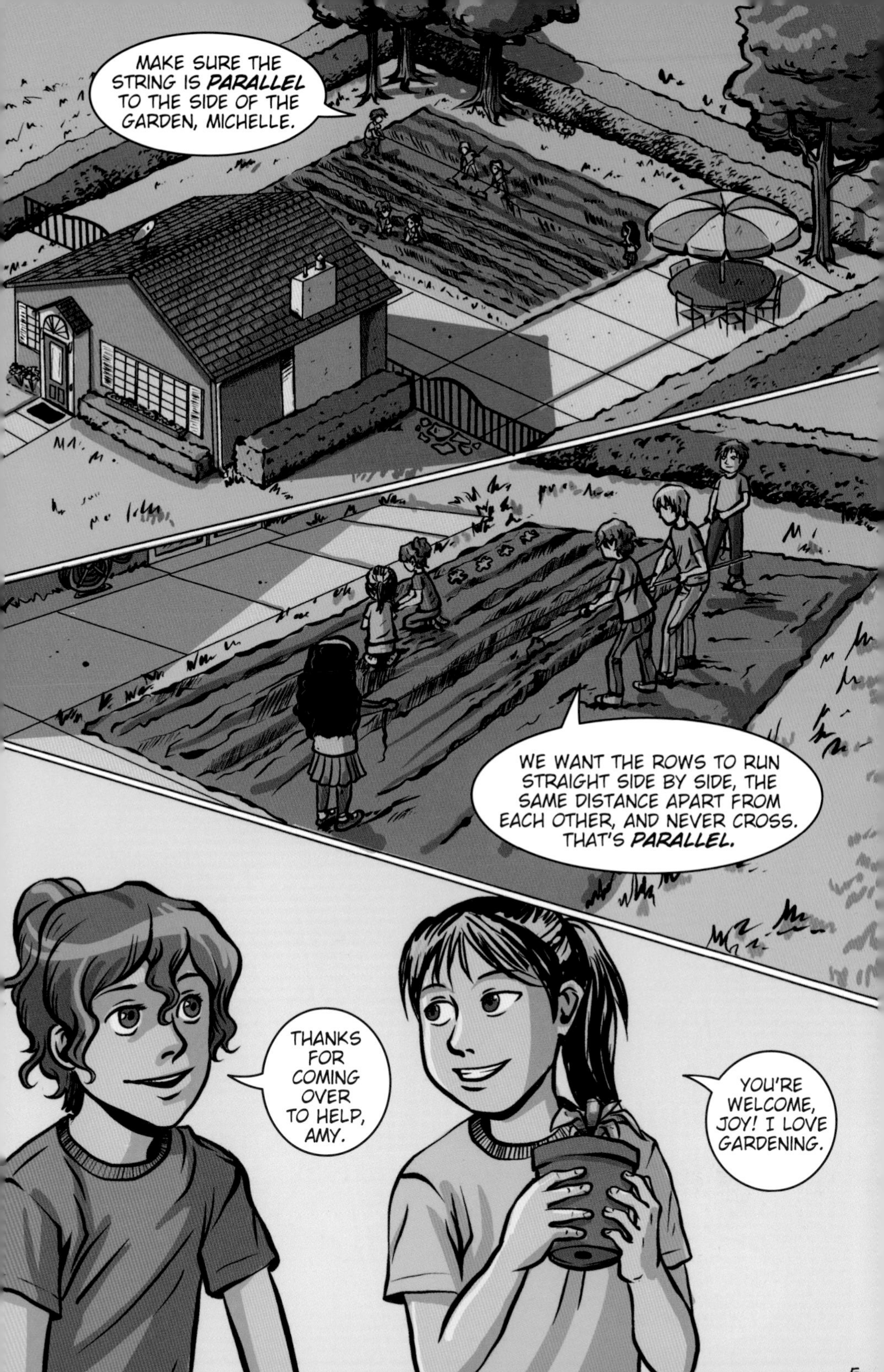
MAKE SURE THE STRING IS PARALLEL TO THE SIDE OF THE GARDEN, MICHELLE.
WE WANT THE ROWS TO RUN STRAIGHT SIDE BY SIDE, THE SAME DISTANCE APART FROM EACH OTHER, AND NEVER CROSS. THAT'S PARALLEL.
THANKS FOR COMING OVER TO HELP, AMY.
YOU'RE WELCOME, JOY! I LOVE GARDENING.

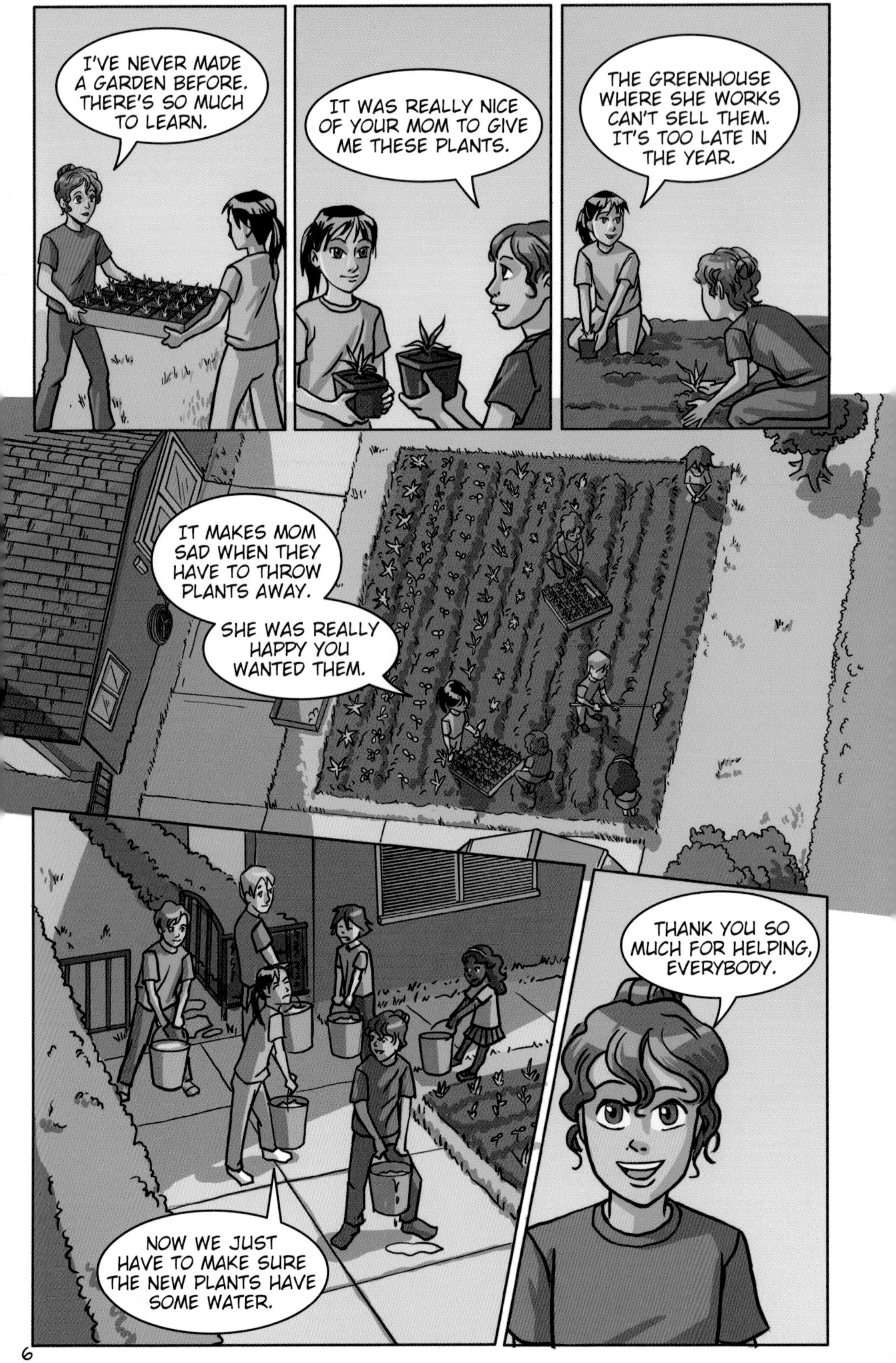
I'VE NEVER MADE A GARDEN BEFORE. THERE'S SO MUCH TO LEARN.
IT WAS REALLY NICE OF YOUR MOM TO GIVE ME THESE PLANTS.
THE GREENHOUSE WHERE SHE WORKS CAN'T SELL THEM. IT'S TOO LATE IN THE YEAR.
IT MAKES MOM SAD WHEN THEY HAVE TO THROW PLANTS AWAY.
SHE WAS REALLY HAPPY YOU WANTED THEM.
NOW WE JUST HAVE TO MAKE SURE THE NEW PLANTS HAVE SOME WATER.
THANK YOU SO MUCH FOR HELPING, EVERYBODY.

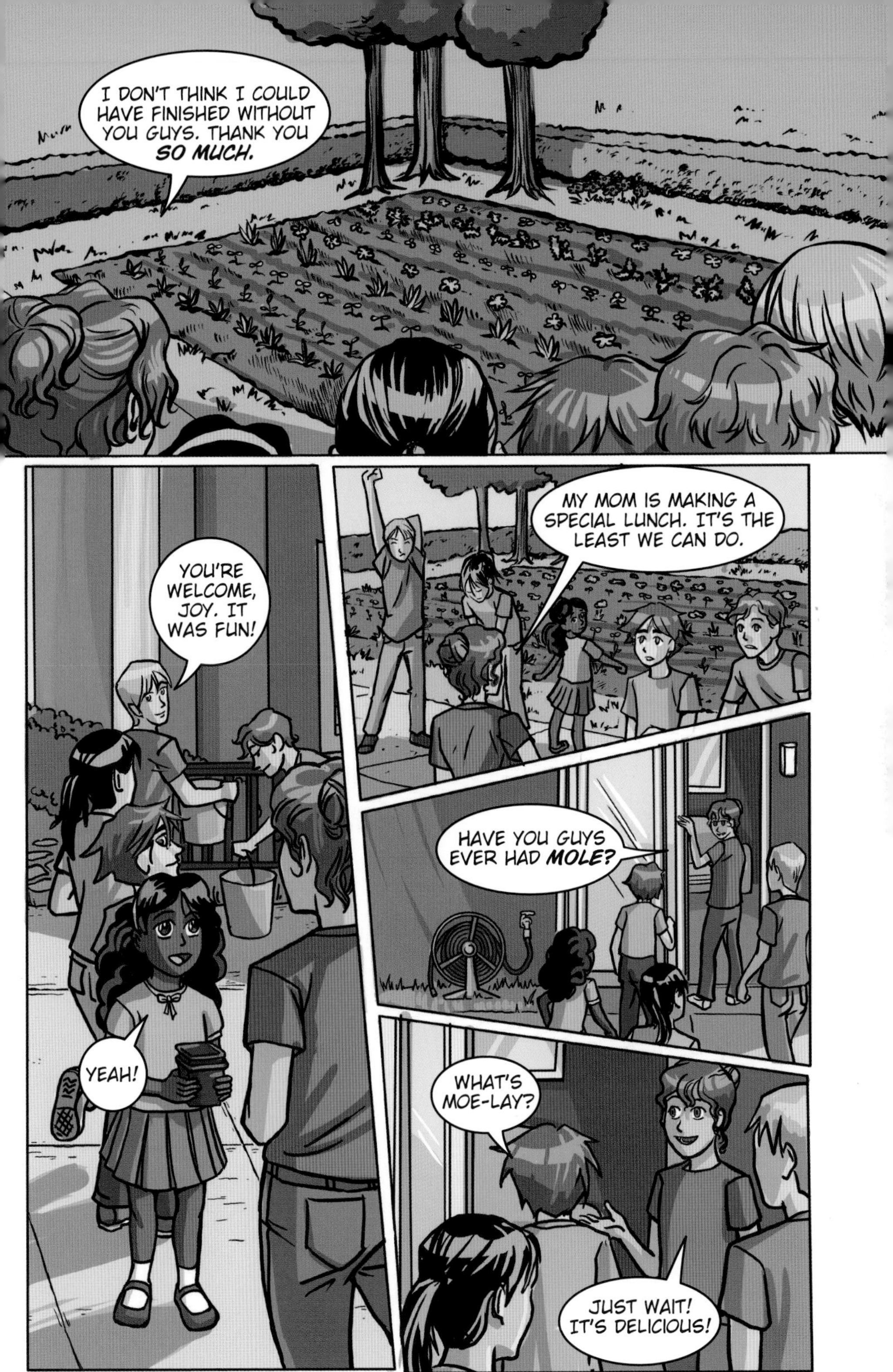
I DON'T THINK I COULD HAVE FINISHED WITHOUT YOU GUYS. THANK YOU ***SO MUCH.***
YOU'RE WELCOME, JOY. IT WAS FUN!
YEAH!
MY MOM IS MAKING A SPECIAL LUNCH. IT'S THE LEAST WE CAN DO.
HAVE YOU GUYS EVER HAD ***MOLE?***
WHAT'S MOE-LAY?
JUST WAIT! IT'S DELICIOUS!

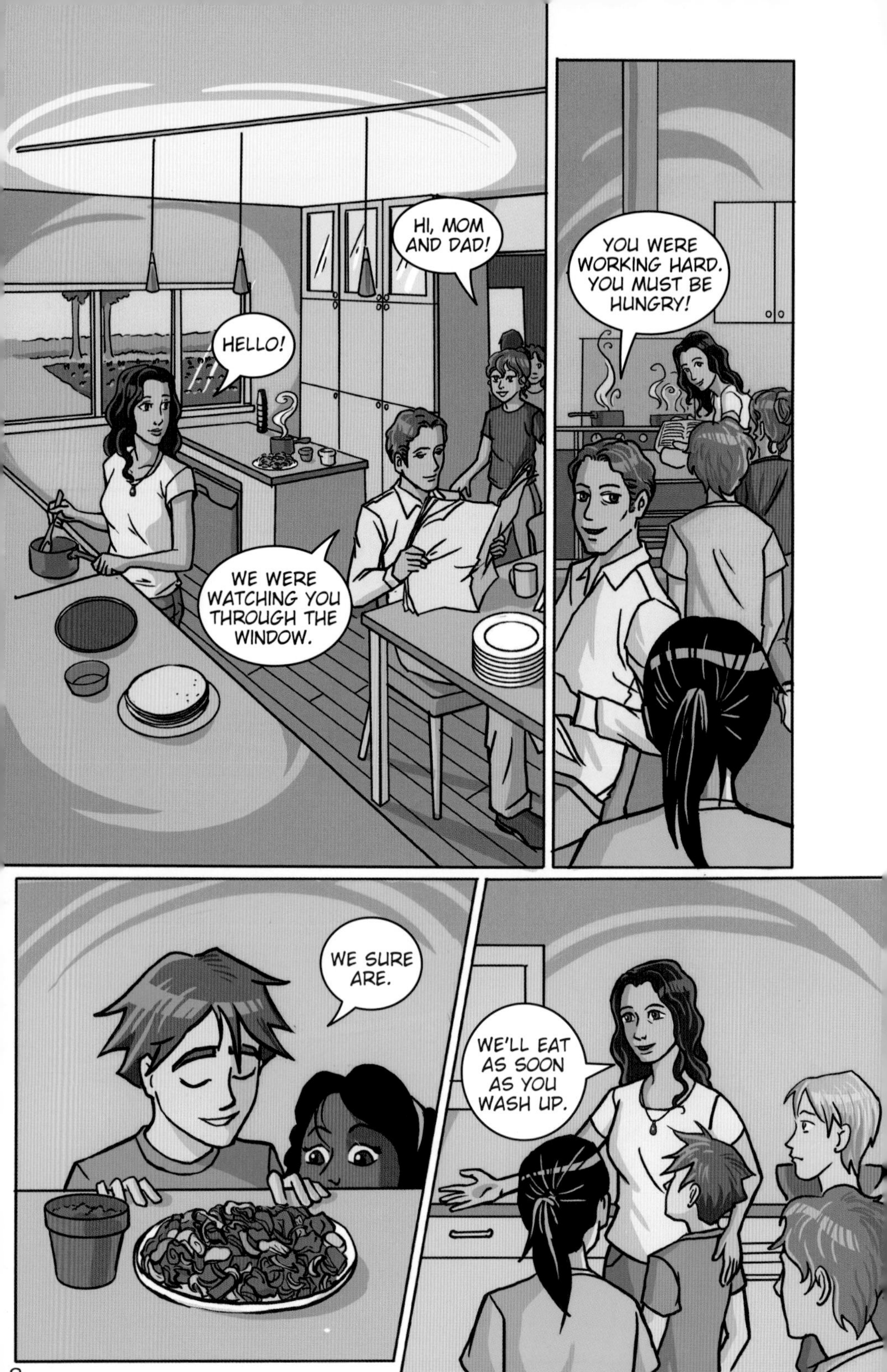
HELLO!
HI, MOM AND DAD!
WE WERE WATCHING YOU THROUGH THE WINDOW.
YOU WERE WORKING HARD. YOU MUST BE HUNGRY!
WE SURE ARE.
WE'LL EAT AS SOON AS YOU WASH UP.

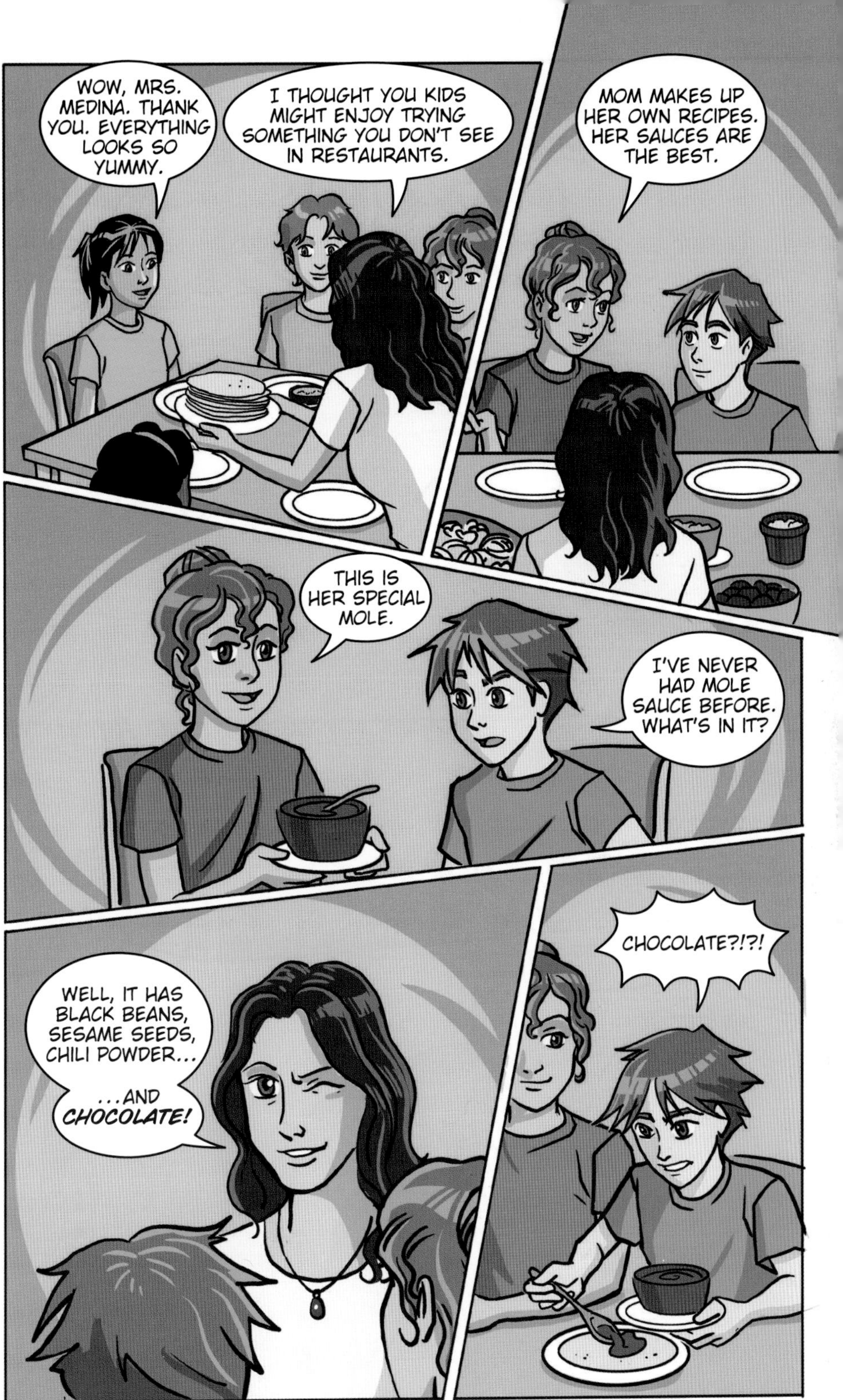
WOW, MRS. MEDINA. THANK YOU. EVERYTHING LOOKS SO YUMMY.
I THOUGHT YOU KIDS MIGHT ENJOY TRYING SOMETHING YOU DON'T SEE IN RESTAURANTS.
MOM MAKES UP HER OWN RECIPES. HER SAUCES ARE THE BEST.
THIS IS HER SPECIAL MOLE.
I'VE NEVER HAD MOLE SAUCE BEFORE. WHAT'S IN IT?
WELL, IT HAS BLACK BEANS, SESAME SEEDS, CHILI POWDER...
...AND ***CHOCOLATE!***
CHOCOLATE?!?!

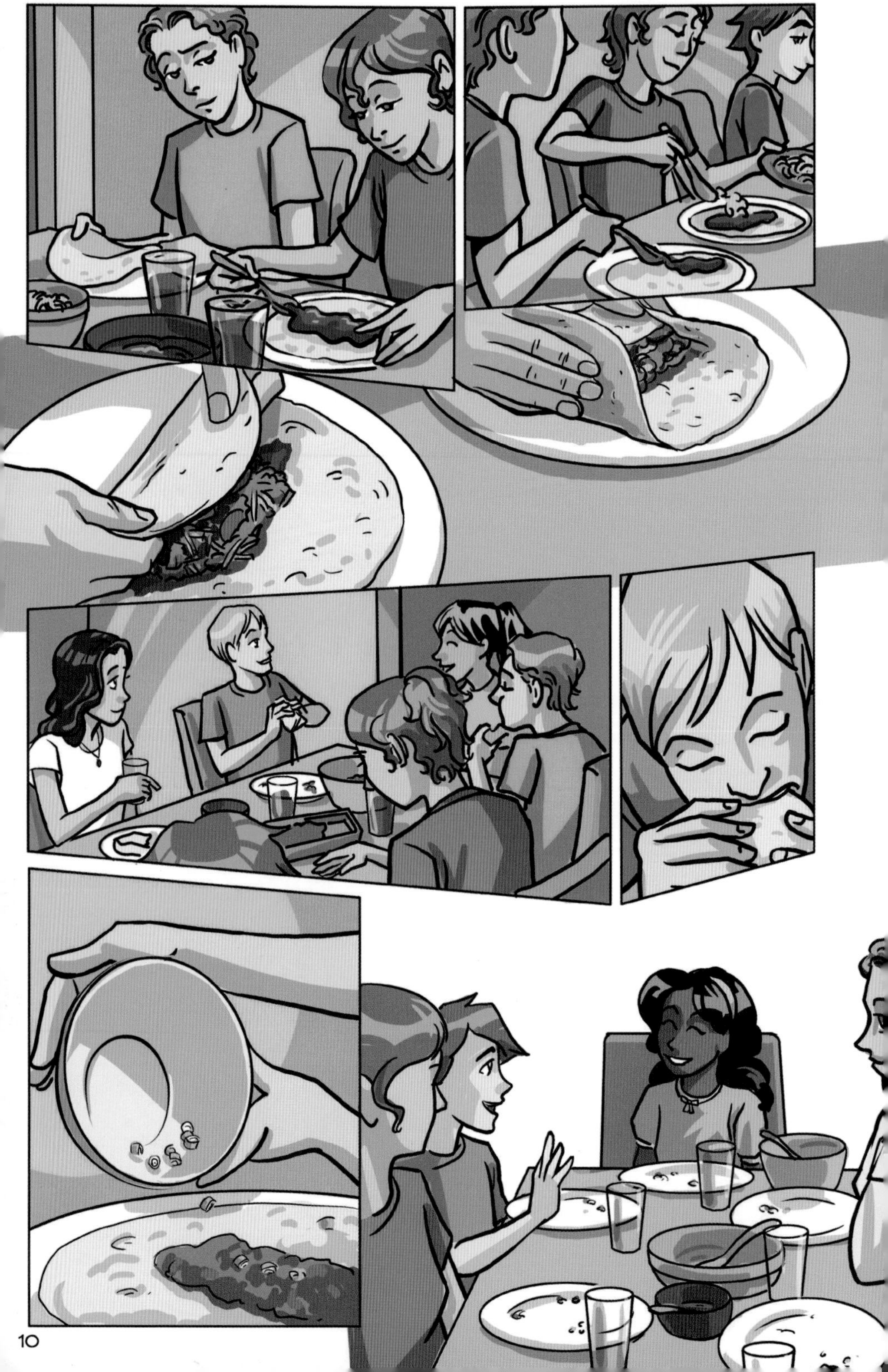

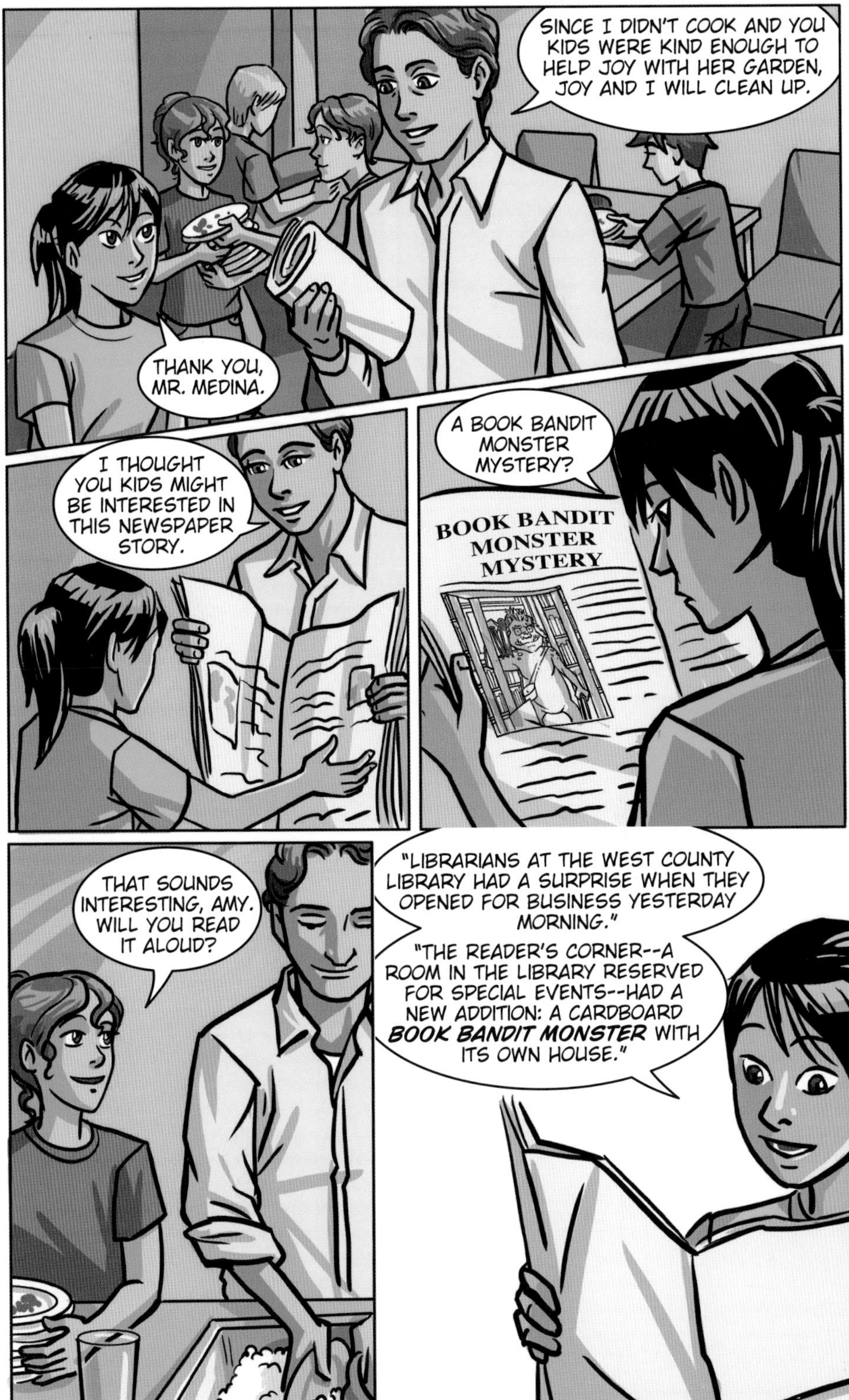
SINCE I DIDN'T COOK AND YOU KIDS WERE KIND ENOUGH TO HELP JOY WITH HER GARDEN, JOY AND I WILL CLEAN UP.
THANK YOU, MR. MEDINA.
I THOUGHT YOU KIDS MIGHT BE INTERESTED IN THIS NEWSPAPER STORY.
A BOOK BANDIT MONSTER MYSTERY?
BOOK BANDIT MONSTER MYSTERY
THAT SOUNDS INTERESTING, AMY. WILL YOU READ IT ALOUD?
"LIBRARIANS AT THE WEST COUNTY LIBRARY HAD A SURPRISE WHEN THEY OPENED FOR BUSINESS YESTERDAY MORNING."
"THE READER'S CORNER--A ROOM IN THE LIBRARY RESERVED FOR SPECIAL EVENTS--HAD A NEW ADDITION: A CARDBOARD ***BOOK BANDIT MONSTER*** WITH ITS OWN HOUSE."

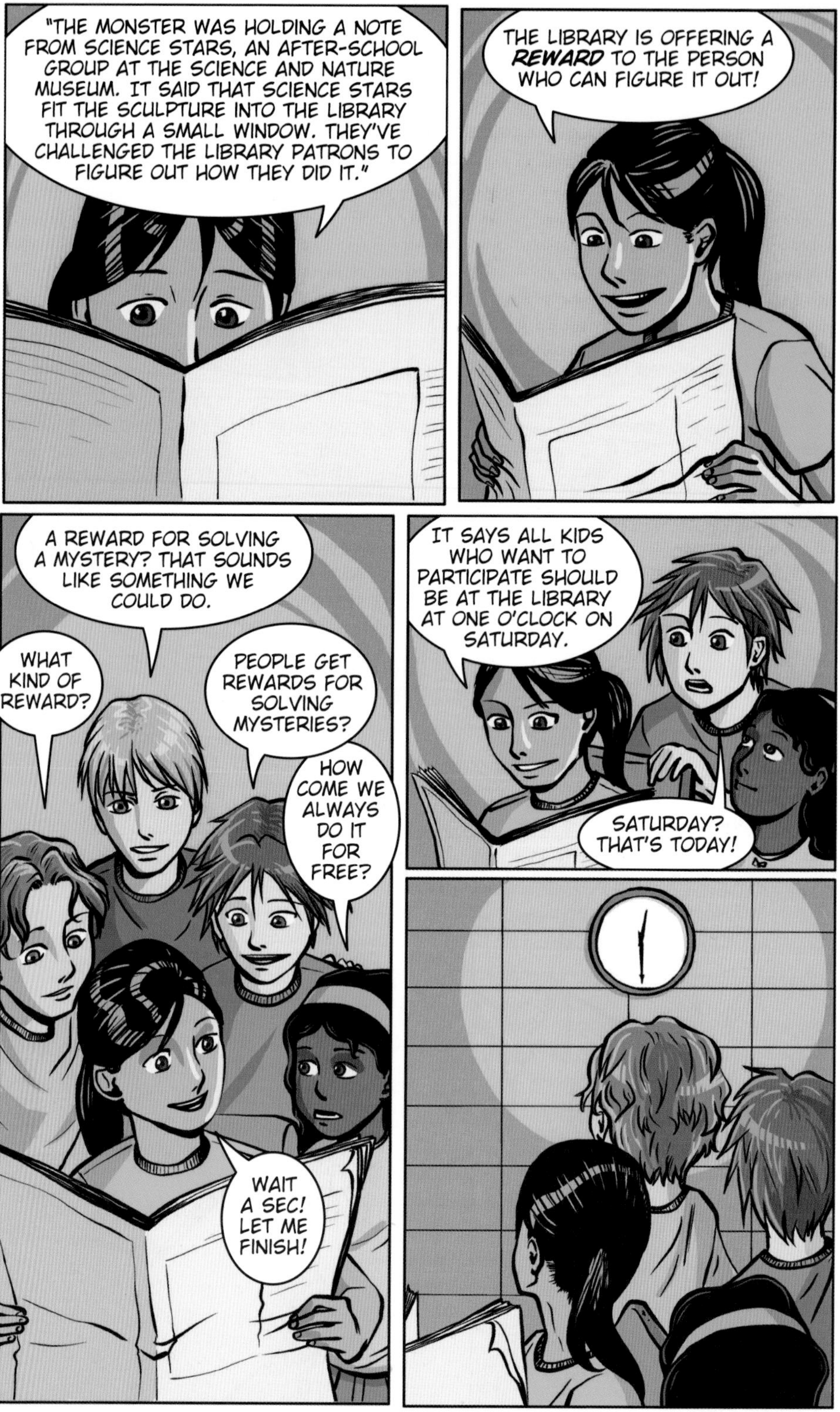
"THE MONSTER WAS HOLDING A NOTE FROM SCIENCE STARS, AN AFTER-SCHOOL GROUP AT THE SCIENCE AND NATURE MUSEUM. IT SAID THAT SCIENCE STARS FIT THE SCULPTURE INTO THE LIBRARY THROUGH A SMALL WINDOW. THEY'VE CHALLENGED THE LIBRARY PATRONS TO FIGURE OUT HOW THEY DID IT."
THE LIBRARY IS OFFERING A ***REWARD*** TO THE PERSON WHO CAN FIGURE IT OUT!
A REWARD FOR SOLVING A MYSTERY? THAT SOUNDS LIKE SOMETHING WE COULD DO.
WHAT KIND OF REWARD?
PEOPLE GET REWARDS FOR SOLVING MYSTERIES?
HOW COME WE ALWAYS DO IT FOR FREE?
WAIT A SEC! LET ME FINISH!
IT SAYS ALL KIDS WHO WANT TO PARTICIPATE SHOULD BE AT THE LIBRARY AT ONE O'CLOCK ON SATURDAY.
SATURDAY? THAT'S TODAY!

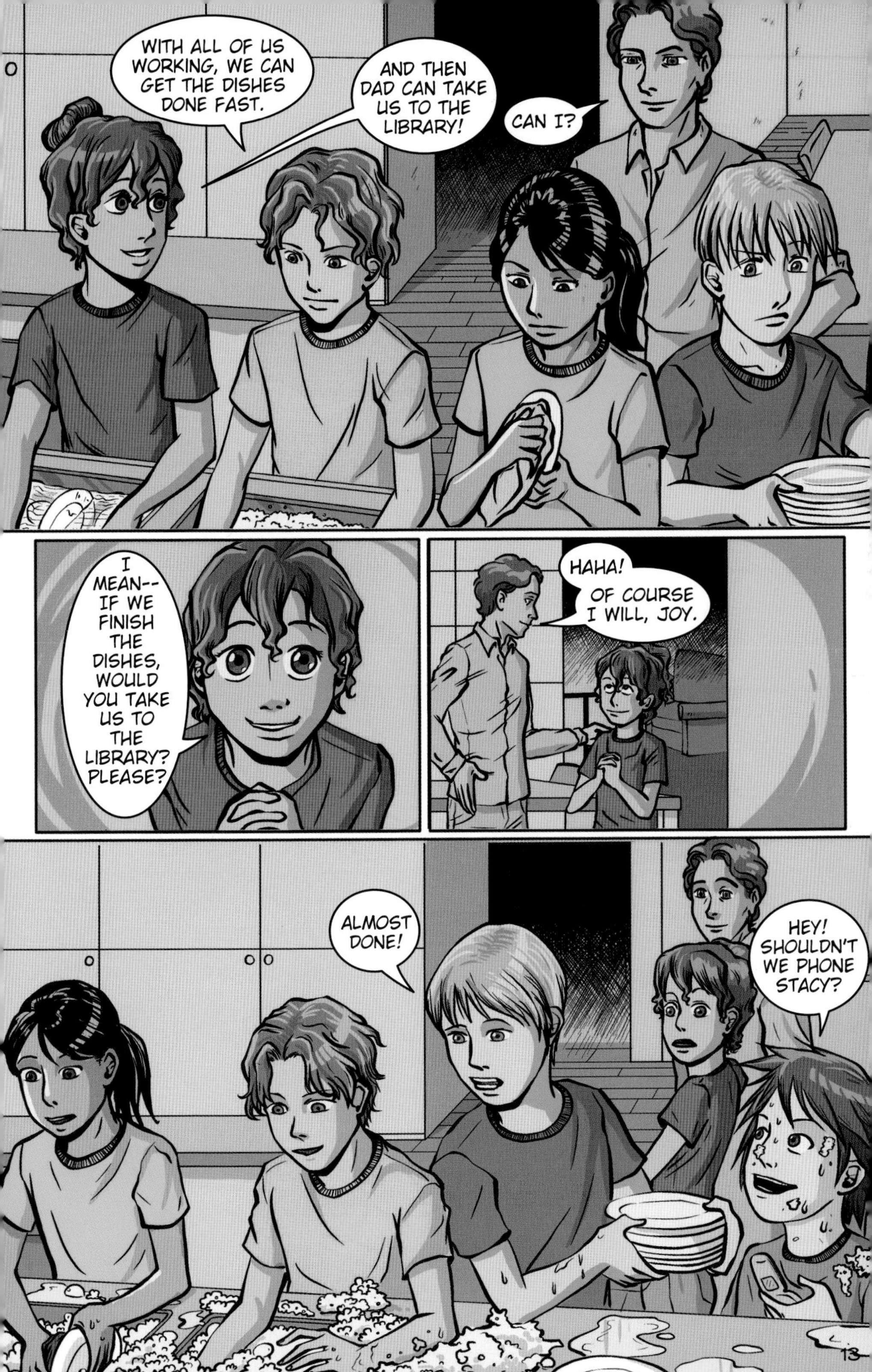
WITH ALL OF US WORKING, WE CAN GET THE DISHES DONE FAST.
AND THEN DAD CAN TAKE US TO THE LIBRARY!
CAN I?
I MEAN-- IF WE FINISH THE DISHES, WOULD YOU TAKE US TO THE LIBRARY? PLEASE?
HAHA!
OF COURSE I WILL, JOY.
ALMOST DONE!
HEY! SHOULDN'T WE PHONE STACY?

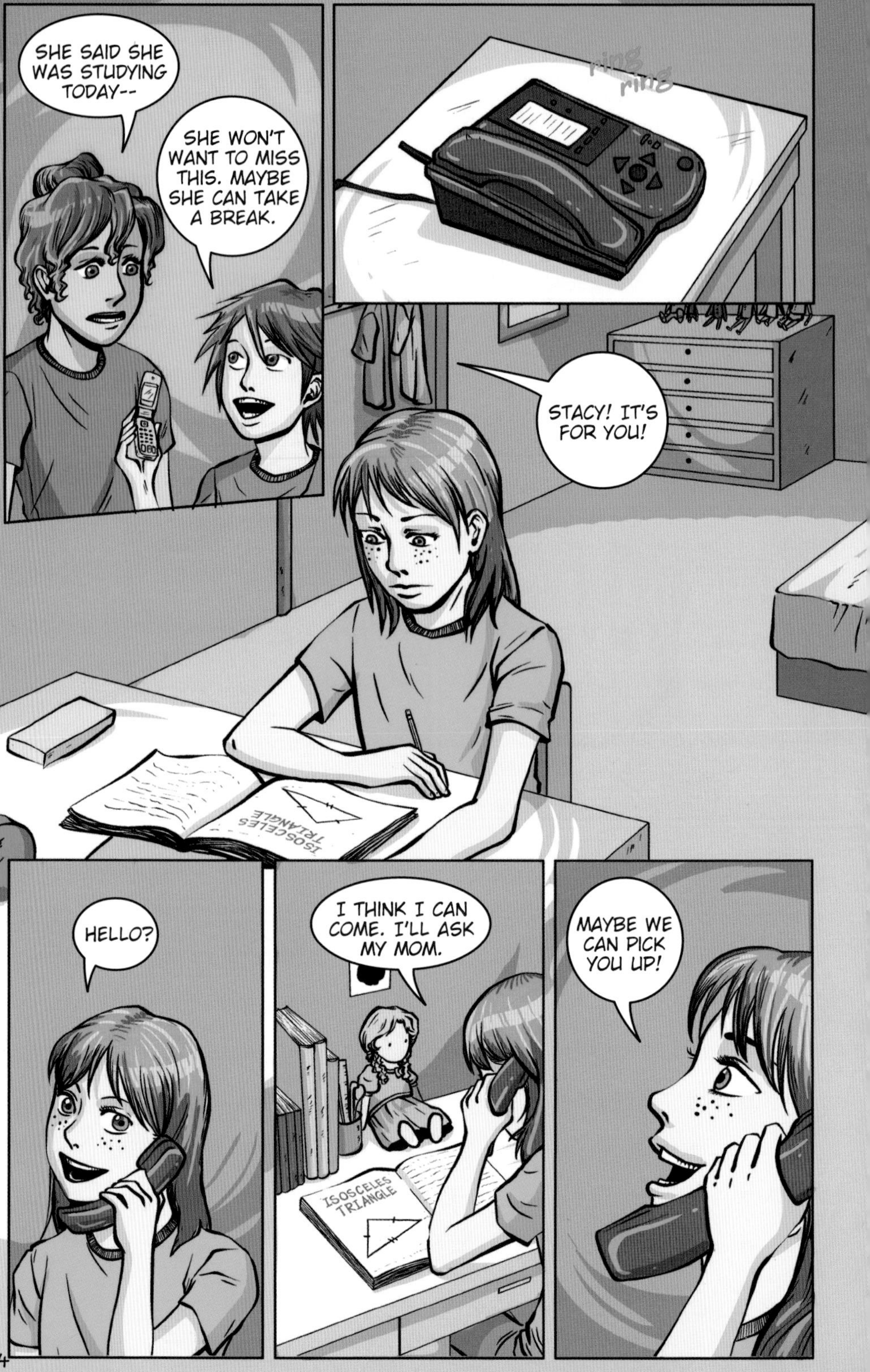
SHE SAID SHE WAS STUDYING TODAY--
SHE WON'T WANT TO MISS THIS. MAYBE SHE CAN TAKE A BREAK.
ring ring
STACY! IT'S FOR YOU!
ISOSCELES TRIANGLE
HELLO?
I THINK I CAN COME. I'LL ASK MY MOM.
ISOSCELES TRIANGLE
MAYBE WE CAN PICK YOU UP!

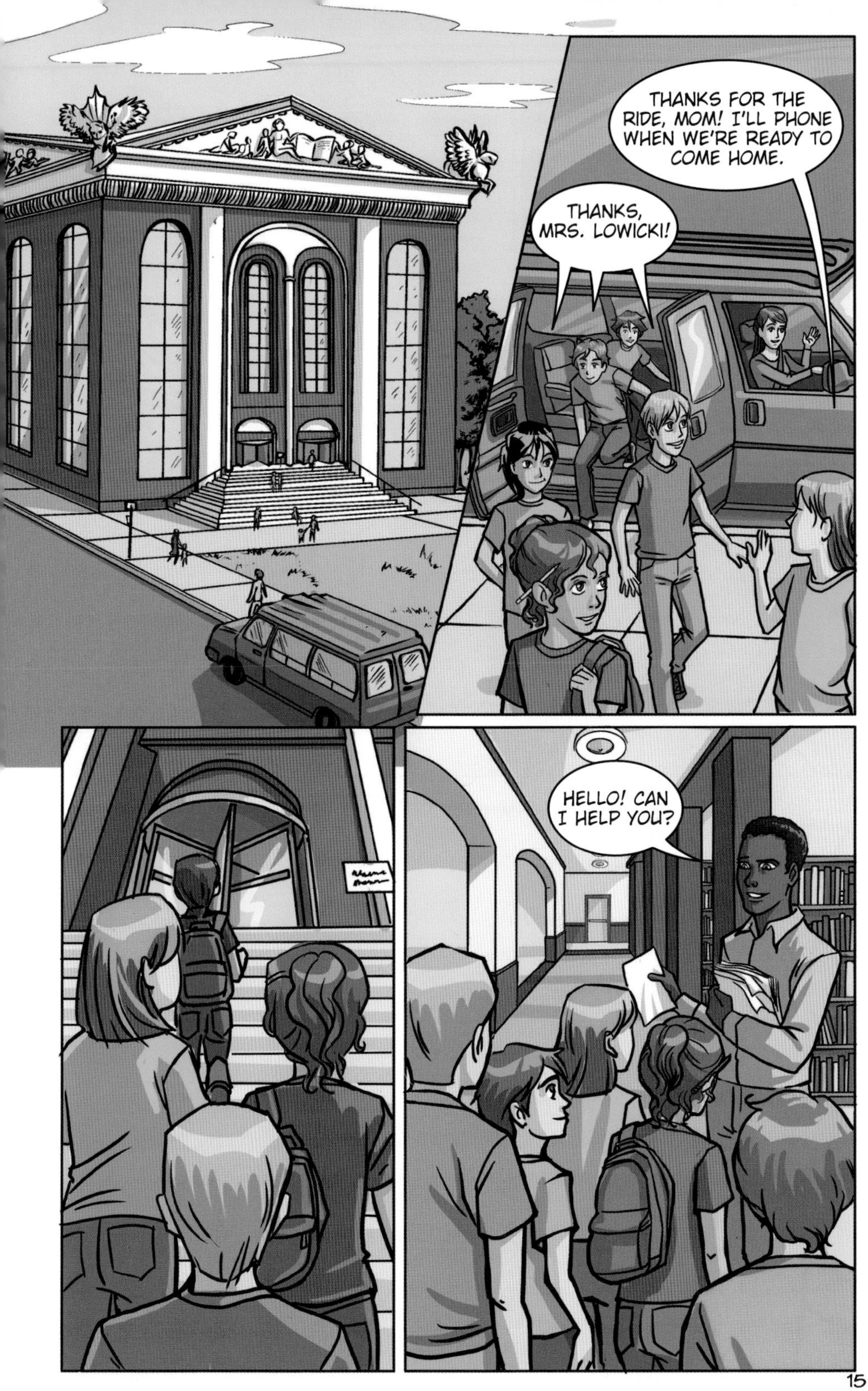
THANKS FOR THE RIDE, MOM! I'LL PHONE WHEN WE'RE READY TO COME HOME.
THANKS, MRS. LOWICKI!
HELLO! CAN I HELP YOU?

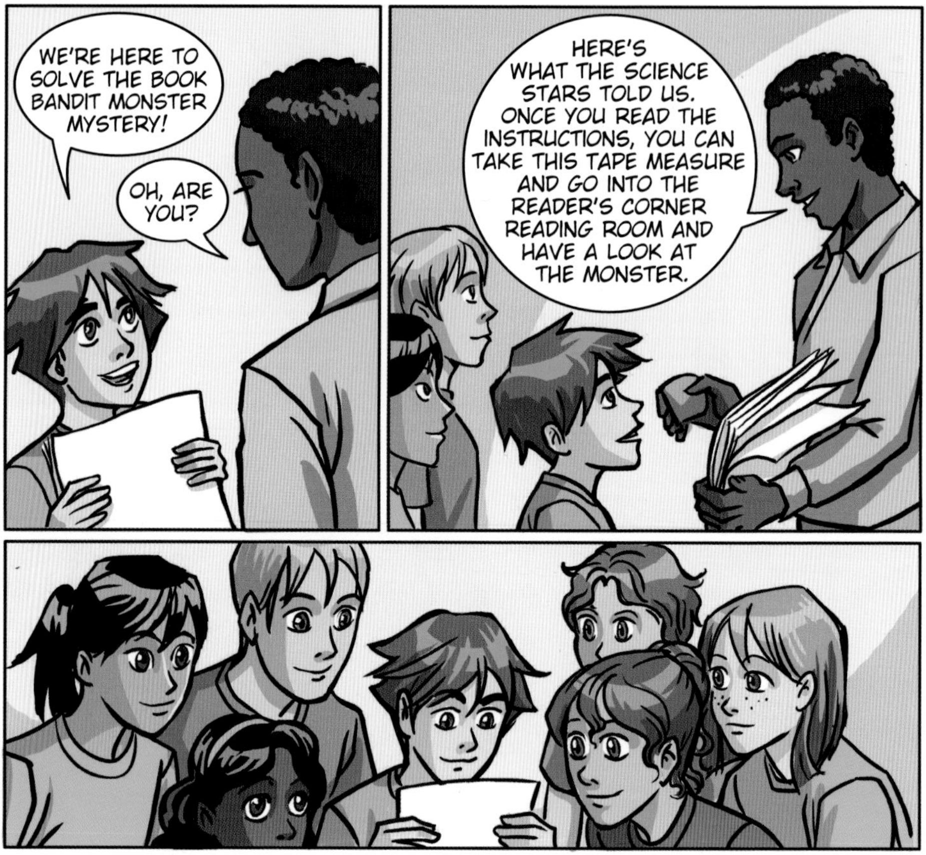
WE'RE HERE TO SOLVE THE BOOK BANDIT MONSTER MYSTERY!
OH, ARE YOU?
HERE'S WHAT THE SCIENCE STARS TOLD US. ONCE YOU READ THE INSTRUCTIONS, YOU CAN TAKE THIS TAPE MEASURE AND GO INTO THE READER'S CORNER READING ROOM AND HAVE A LOOK AT THE MONSTER.

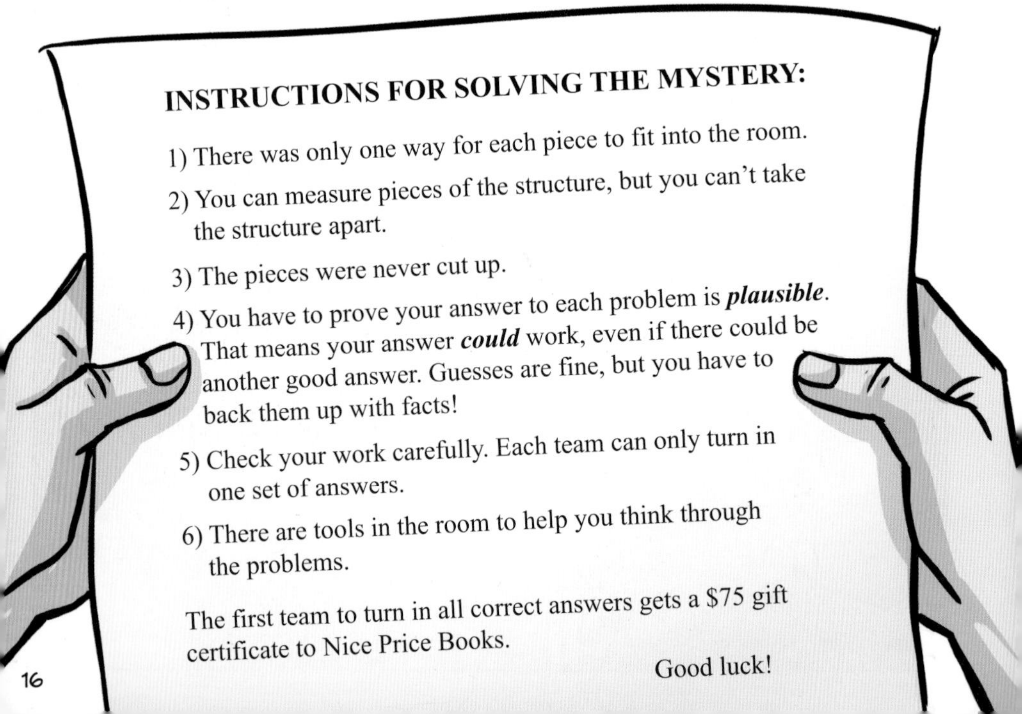

INSTRUCTIONS FOR SOLVING THE MYSTERY:

1) There was only one way for each piece to fit into the room.
2) You can measure pieces of the structure, but you can't take the structure apart.
3) The pieces were never cut up.
4) You have to prove your answer to each problem is ***plausible***. That means your answer ***could*** work, even if there could be another good answer. Guesses are fine, but you have to back them up with facts!
5) Check your work carefully. Each team can only turn in one set of answers.
6) There are tools in the room to help you think through the problems.

The first team to turn in all correct answers gets a $75 gift certificate to Nice Price Books.

Good luck!

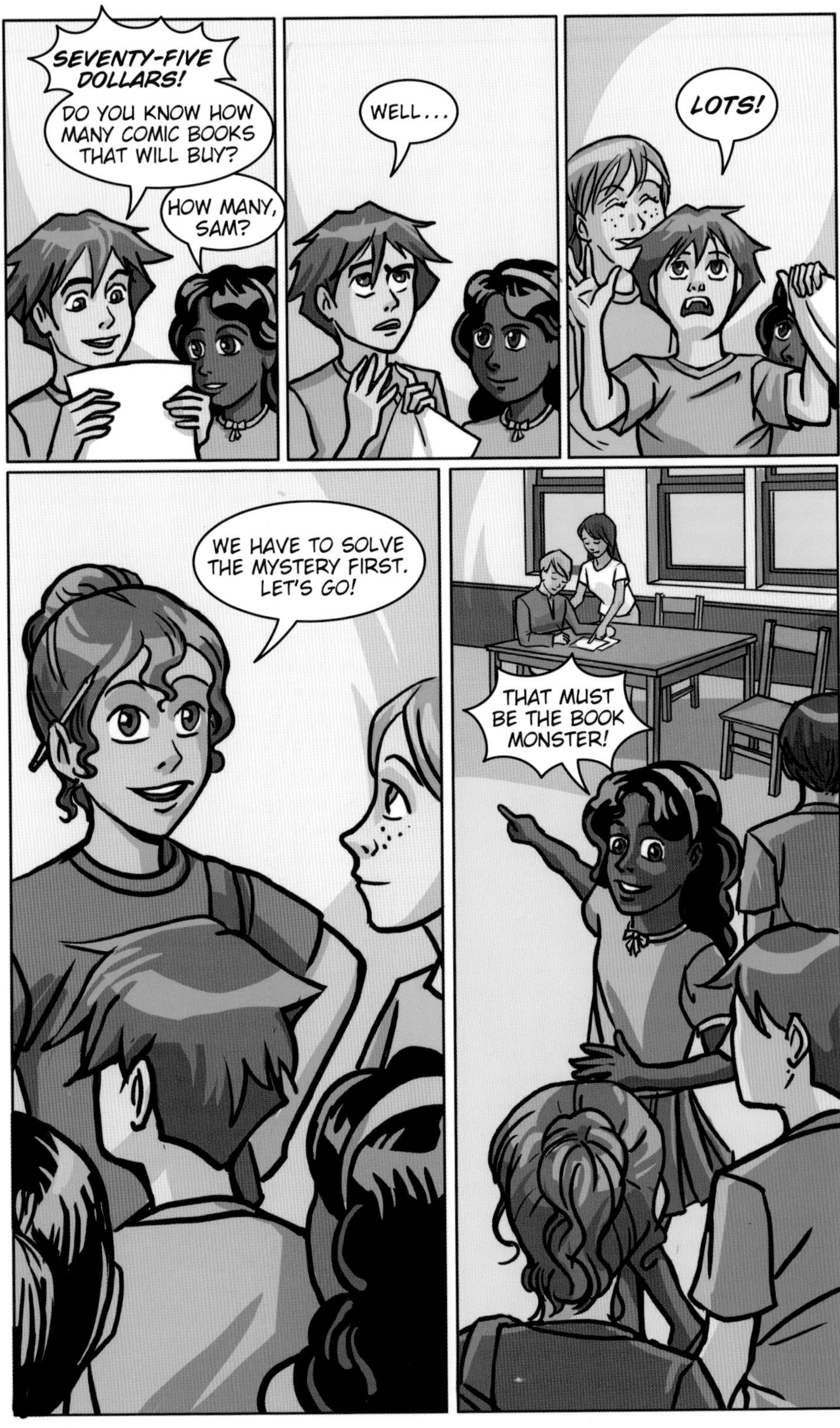
SEVENTY-FIVE DOLLARS!
DO YOU KNOW HOW MANY COMIC BOOKS THAT WILL BUY?
HOW MANY, SAM?
WELL . . .
LOTS!
WE HAVE TO SOLVE THE MYSTERY FIRST. LET'S GO!
THAT MUST BE THE BOOK MONSTER!

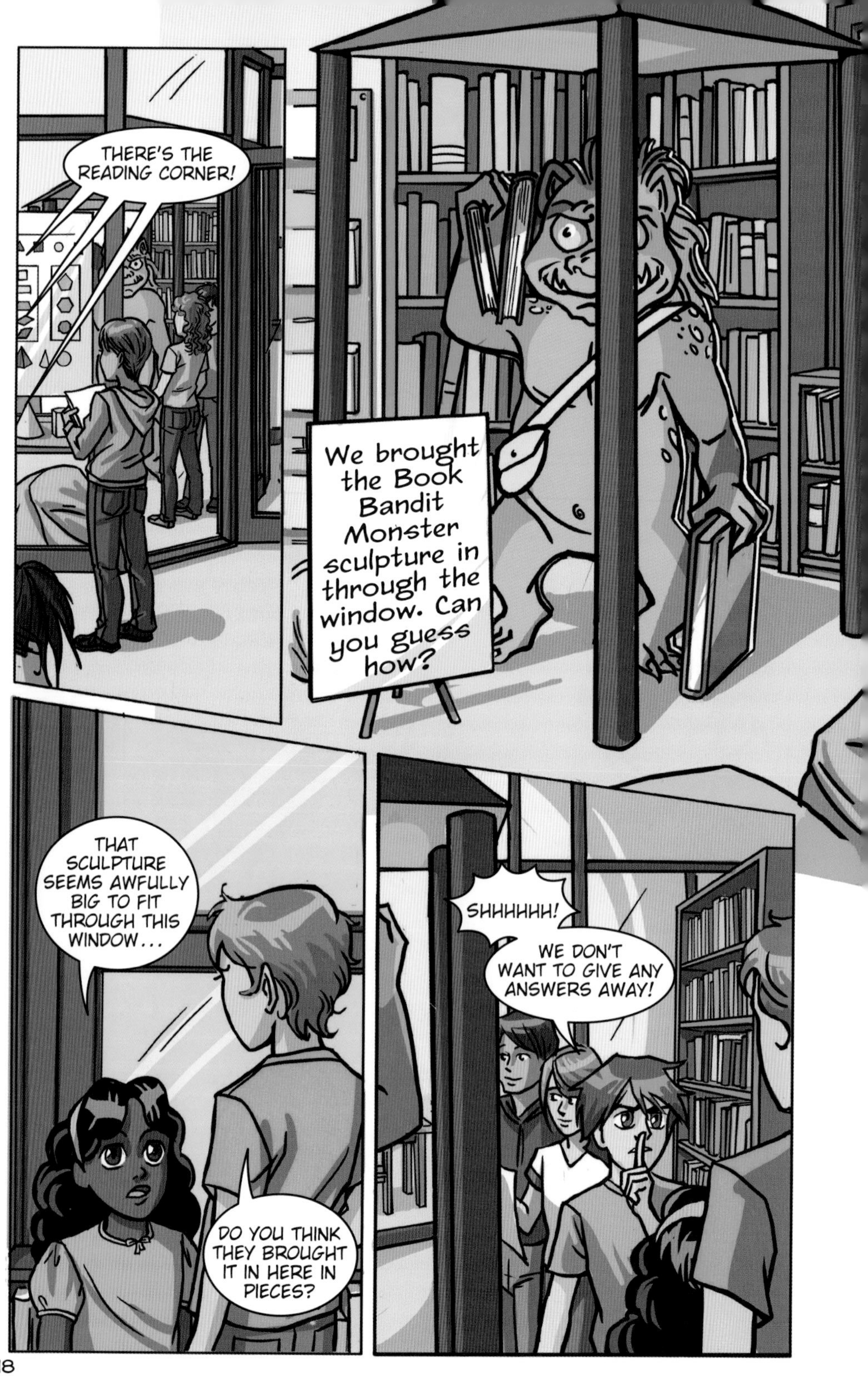
THERE'S THE READING CORNER!
We brought the Book Bandit Monster sculpture in through the window. Can you guess how?
THAT SCULPTURE SEEMS AWFULLY BIG TO FIT THROUGH THIS WINDOW...
DO YOU THINK THEY BROUGHT IT IN HERE IN PIECES?
SHHHHHH!
WE DON'T WANT TO GIVE ANY ANSWERS AWAY!

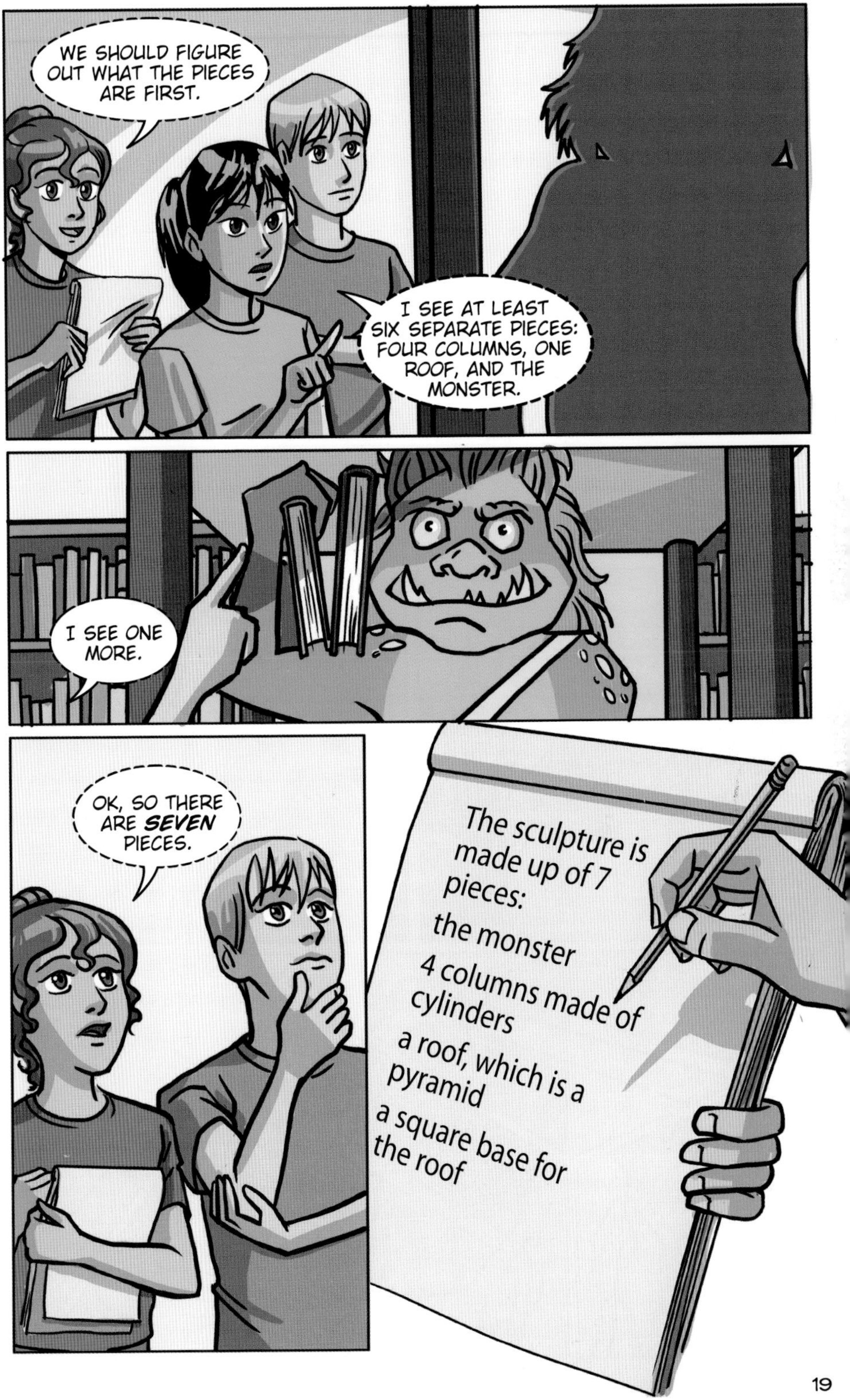
WE SHOULD FIGURE OUT WHAT THE PIECES ARE FIRST.
I SEE AT LEAST SIX SEPARATE PIECES: FOUR COLUMNS, ONE ROOF, AND THE MONSTER.
I SEE ONE MORE.
OK, SO THERE ARE ***SEVEN*** PIECES.
The sculpture is made up of 7 pieces:
the monster
4 columns made of cylinders
a roof, which is a pyramid
a square base for the roof

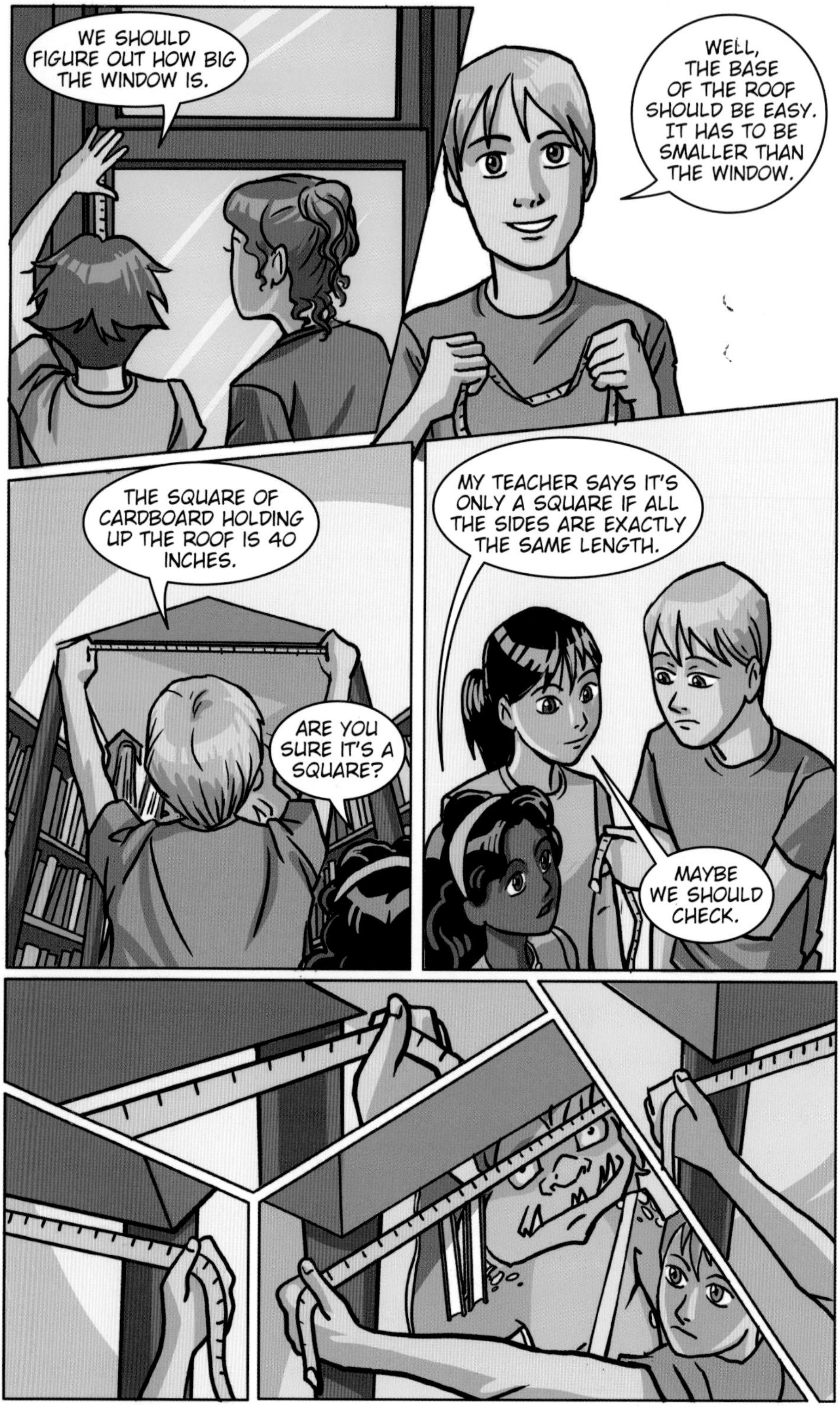
WE SHOULD FIGURE OUT HOW BIG THE WINDOW IS.
WELL, THE BASE OF THE ROOF SHOULD BE EASY. IT HAS TO BE SMALLER THAN THE WINDOW.
THE SQUARE OF CARDBOARD HOLDING UP THE ROOF IS 40 INCHES.
ARE YOU SURE IT'S A SQUARE?
MY TEACHER SAYS IT'S ONLY A SQUARE IF ALL THE SIDES ARE EXACTLY THE SAME LENGTH.
MAYBE WE SHOULD CHECK.

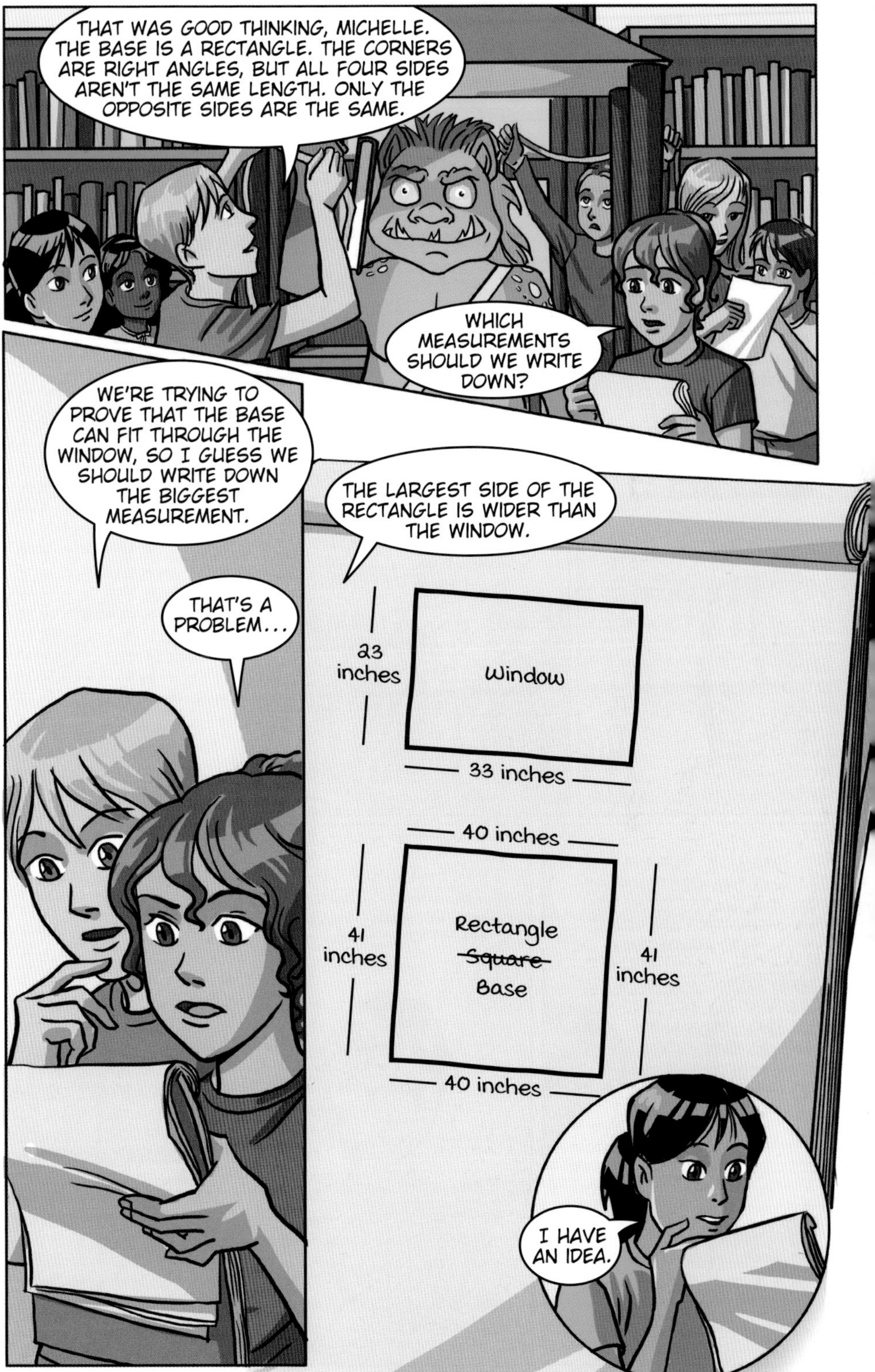
THAT WAS GOOD THINKING, MICHELLE. THE BASE IS A RECTANGLE. THE CORNERS ARE RIGHT ANGLES, BUT ALL FOUR SIDES AREN'T THE SAME LENGTH. ONLY THE OPPOSITE SIDES ARE THE SAME.
WHICH MEASUREMENTS SHOULD WE WRITE DOWN?
WE'RE TRYING TO PROVE THAT THE BASE CAN FIT THROUGH THE WINDOW, SO I GUESS WE SHOULD WRITE DOWN THE BIGGEST MEASUREMENT.
THE LARGEST SIDE OF THE RECTANGLE IS WIDER THAN THE WINDOW.
THAT'S A PROBLEM...
23 inches
Window
33 inches
40 inches
41 inches
Rectangle
~~Square~~
Base
41 inches
40 inches
I HAVE AN IDEA.

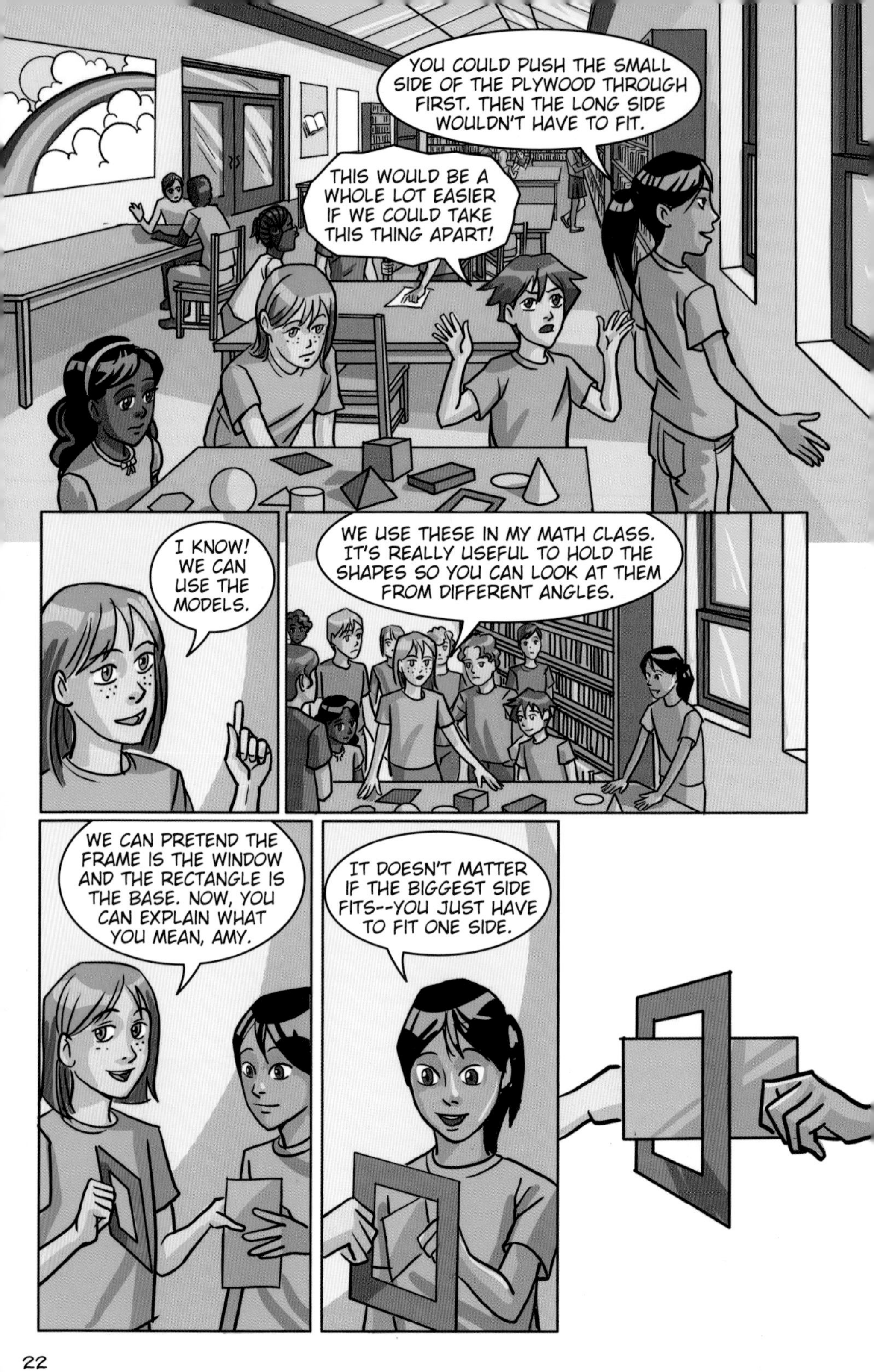
THIS WOULD BE A WHOLE LOT EASIER IF WE COULD TAKE THIS THING APART!
YOU COULD PUSH THE SMALL SIDE OF THE PLYWOOD THROUGH FIRST. THEN THE LONG SIDE WOULDN'T HAVE TO FIT.
I KNOW! WE CAN USE THE MODELS.
WE USE THESE IN MY MATH CLASS. IT'S REALLY USEFUL TO HOLD THE SHAPES SO YOU CAN LOOK AT THEM FROM DIFFERENT ANGLES.
WE CAN PRETEND THE FRAME IS THE WINDOW AND THE RECTANGLE IS THE BASE. NOW, YOU CAN EXPLAIN WHAT YOU MEAN, AMY.
IT DOESN'T MATTER IF THE BIGGEST SIDE FITS--YOU JUST HAVE TO FIT ONE SIDE.

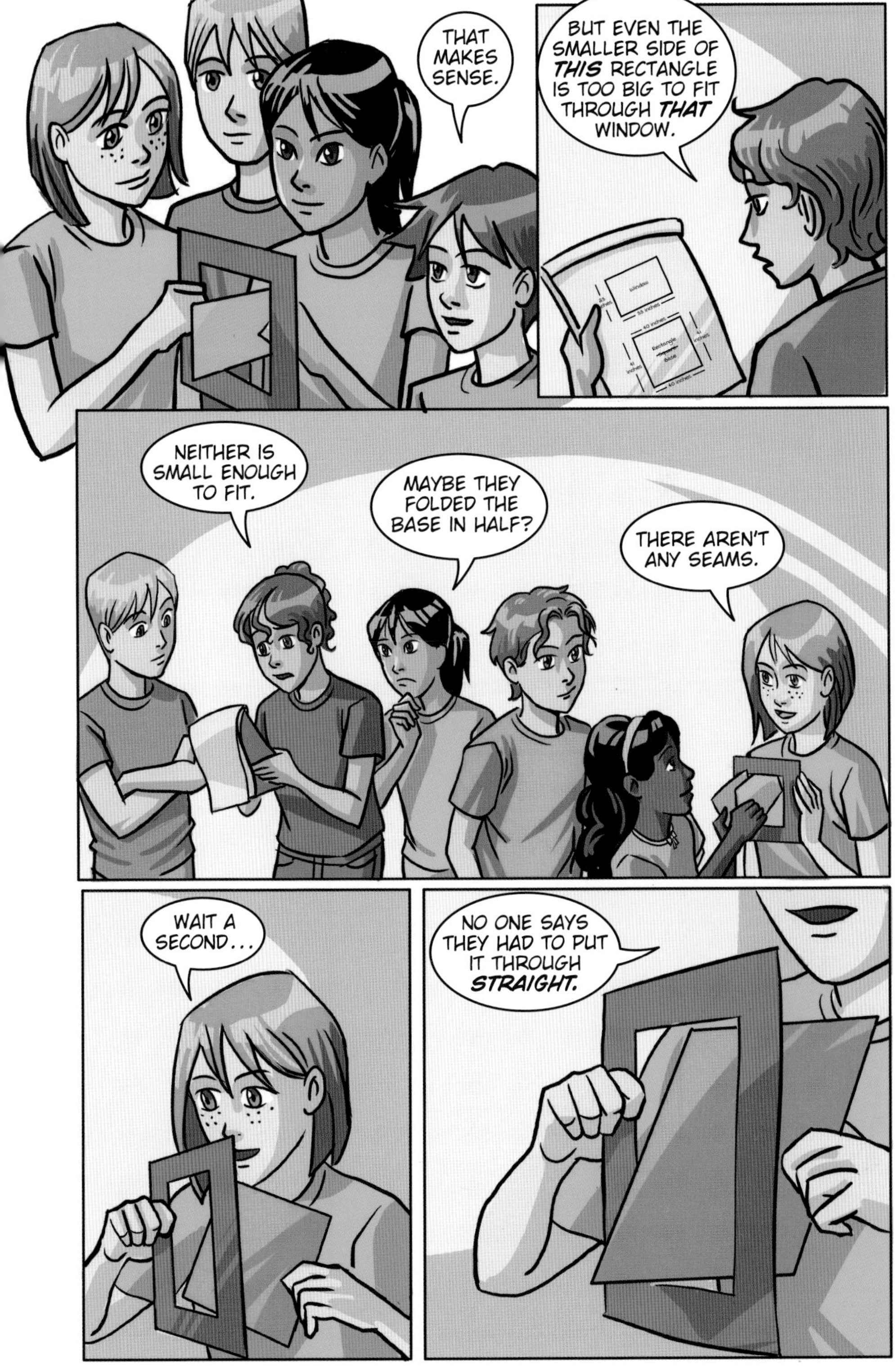
THAT MAKES SENSE.
BUT EVEN THE SMALLER SIDE OF *THIS* RECTANGLE IS TOO BIG TO FIT THROUGH *THAT* WINDOW.
NEITHER IS SMALL ENOUGH TO FIT.
MAYBE THEY FOLDED THE BASE IN HALF?
THERE AREN'T ANY SEAMS.
WAIT A SECOND...
NO ONE SAYS THEY HAD TO PUT IT THROUGH *STRAIGHT.*

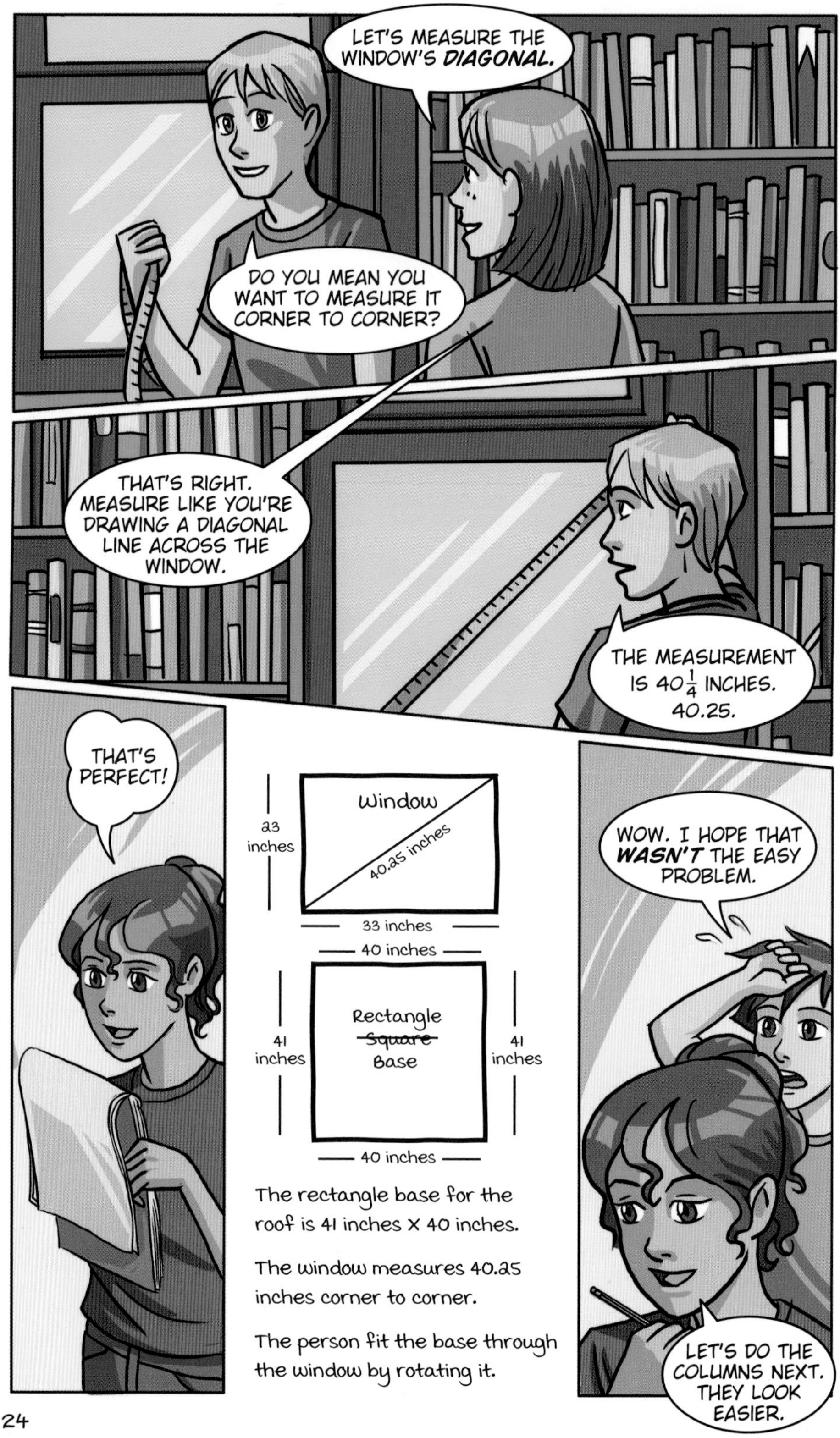
LET'S MEASURE THE WINDOW'S *DIAGONAL.*
DO YOU MEAN YOU WANT TO MEASURE IT CORNER TO CORNER?
THAT'S RIGHT. MEASURE LIKE YOU'RE DRAWING A DIAGONAL LINE ACROSS THE WINDOW.
THE MEASUREMENT IS $40\frac{1}{4}$ INCHES. 40.25.
THAT'S PERFECT!
Window
23 inches
40.25 inches
33 inches
40 inches
Rectangle ~~Square~~ Base
41 inches
41 inches
40 inches
The rectangle base for the roof is 41 inches X 40 inches.
The window measures 40.25 inches corner to corner.
The person fit the base through the window by rotating it.
WOW. I HOPE THAT ***WASN'T*** THE EASY PROBLEM.
LET'S DO THE COLUMNS NEXT. THEY LOOK EASIER.

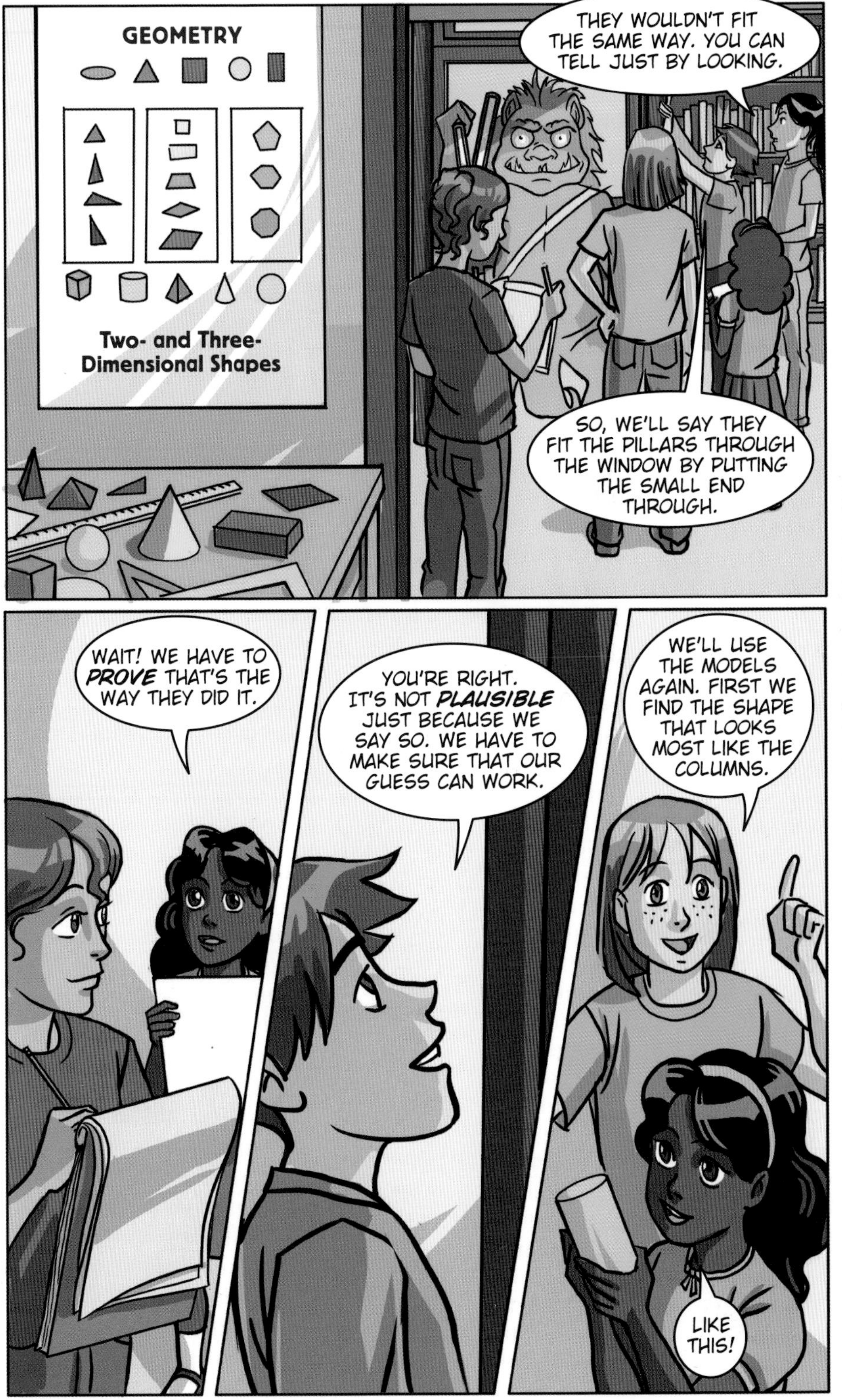
GEOMETRY
Two- and Three-Dimensional Shapes
THEY WOULDN'T FIT THE SAME WAY. YOU CAN TELL JUST BY LOOKING.
SO, WE'LL SAY THEY FIT THE PILLARS THROUGH THE WINDOW BY PUTTING THE SMALL END THROUGH.
WAIT! WE HAVE TO PROVE THAT'S THE WAY THEY DID IT.
YOU'RE RIGHT. IT'S NOT PLAUSIBLE JUST BECAUSE WE SAY SO. WE HAVE TO MAKE SURE THAT OUR GUESS CAN WORK.
WE'LL USE THE MODELS AGAIN. FIRST WE FIND THE SHAPE THAT LOOKS MOST LIKE THE COLUMNS.
LIKE THIS!

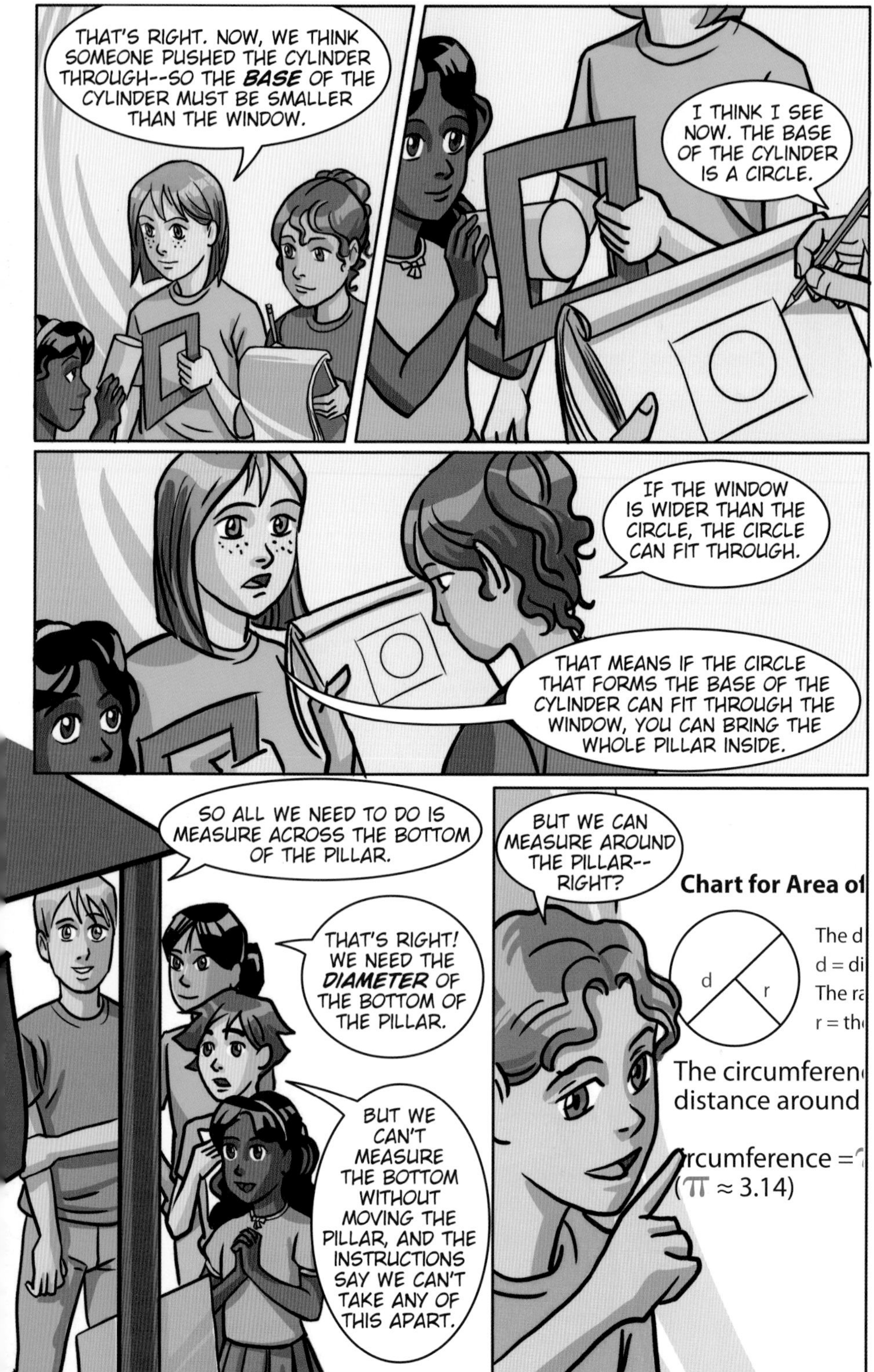

THAT'S RIGHT. NOW, WE THINK SOMEONE PUSHED THE CYLINDER THROUGH--SO THE BASE OF THE CYLINDER MUST BE SMALLER THAN THE WINDOW.
I THINK I SEE NOW. THE BASE OF THE CYLINDER IS A CIRCLE.
IF THE WINDOW IS WIDER THAN THE CIRCLE, THE CIRCLE CAN FIT THROUGH.
THAT MEANS IF THE CIRCLE THAT FORMS THE BASE OF THE CYLINDER CAN FIT THROUGH THE WINDOW, YOU CAN BRING THE WHOLE PILLAR INSIDE.
SO ALL WE NEED TO DO IS MEASURE ACROSS THE BOTTOM OF THE PILLAR.
THAT'S RIGHT! WE NEED THE DIAMETER OF THE BOTTOM OF THE PILLAR.
BUT WE CAN'T MEASURE THE BOTTOM WITHOUT MOVING THE PILLAR, AND THE INSTRUCTIONS SAY WE CAN'T TAKE ANY OF THIS APART.
BUT WE CAN MEASURE AROUND THE PILLAR--RIGHT?
Chart for Area of
The d
d = di
The ra
r = th
d
r
The circumferen
distance around
rcumference =
(π ≈ 3.14)

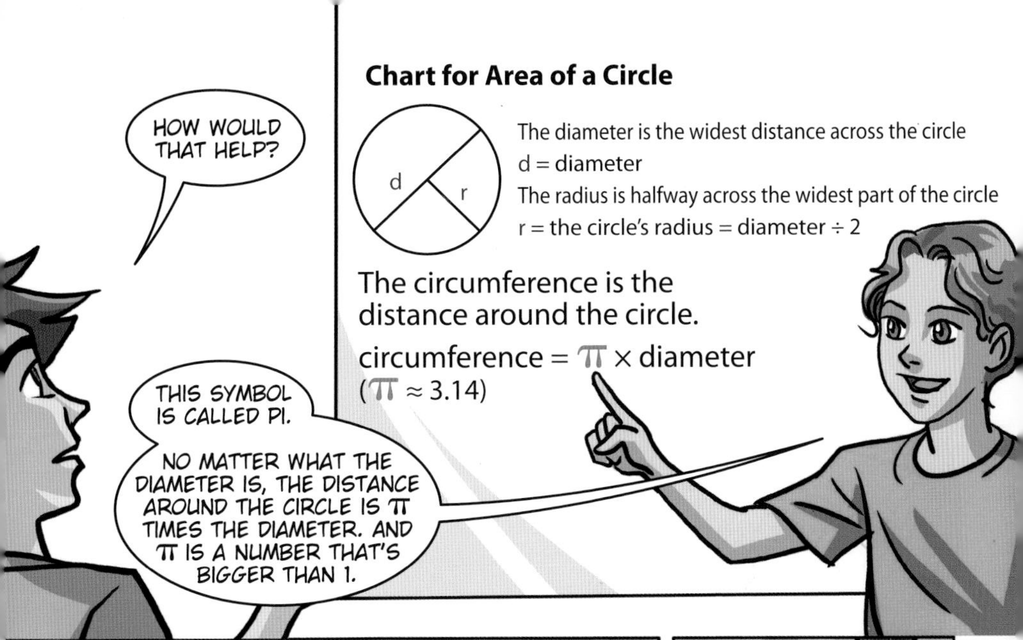
HOW WOULD THAT HELP?
Chart for Area of a Circle
d
r
The diameter is the widest distance across the circle
d = diameter
The radius is halfway across the widest part of the circle
r = the circle's radius = diameter ÷ 2
The circumference is the distance around the circle.
circumference = π × diameter
(π ≈ 3.14)
THIS SYMBOL IS CALLED PI.
NO MATTER WHAT THE DIAMETER IS, THE DISTANCE AROUND THE CIRCLE IS π TIMES THE DIAMETER. AND π IS A NUMBER THAT'S BIGGER THAN 1.
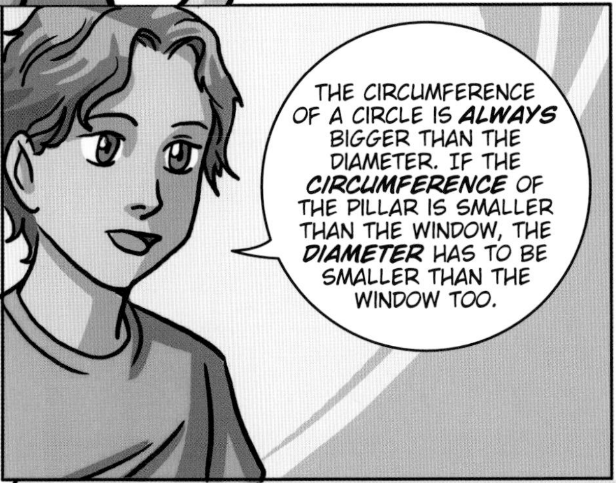
THE CIRCUMFERENCE OF A CIRCLE IS ALWAYS BIGGER THAN THE DIAMETER. IF THE CIRCUMFERENCE OF THE PILLAR IS SMALLER THAN THE WINDOW, THE DIAMETER HAS TO BE SMALLER THAN THE WINDOW TOO.
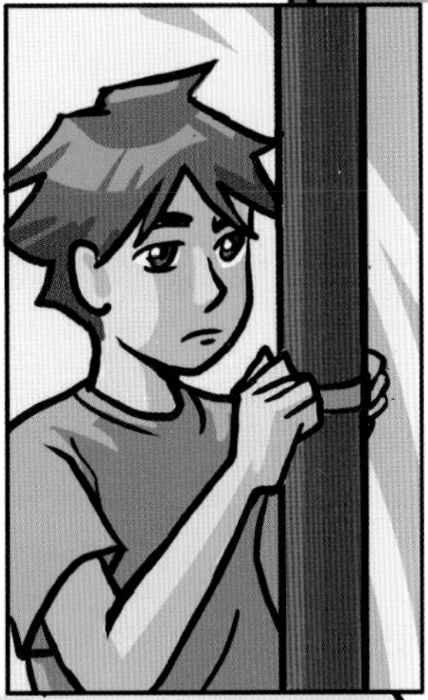
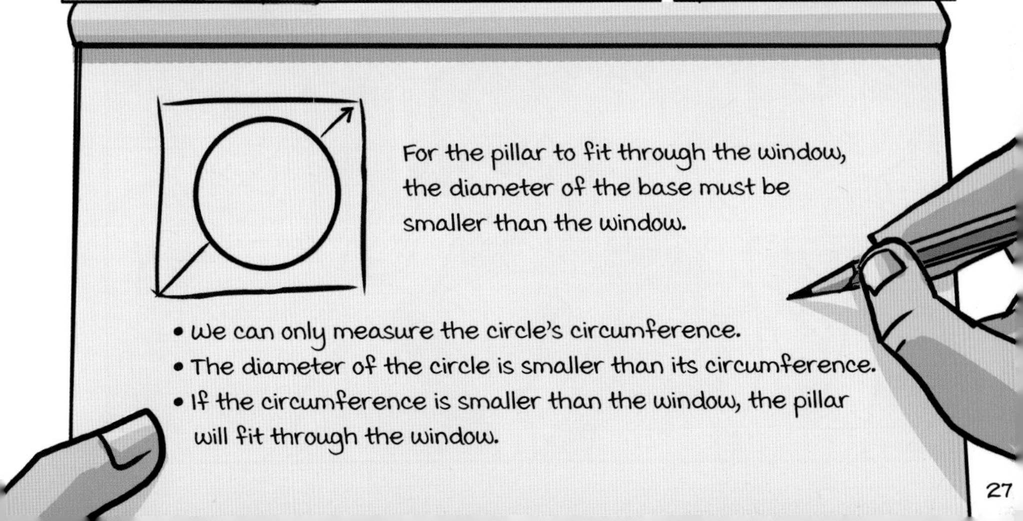
For the pillar to fit through the window, the diameter of the base must be smaller than the window.
• We can only measure the circle's circumference.
• The diameter of the circle is smaller than its circumference.
• If the circumference is smaller than the window, the pillar will fit through the window.

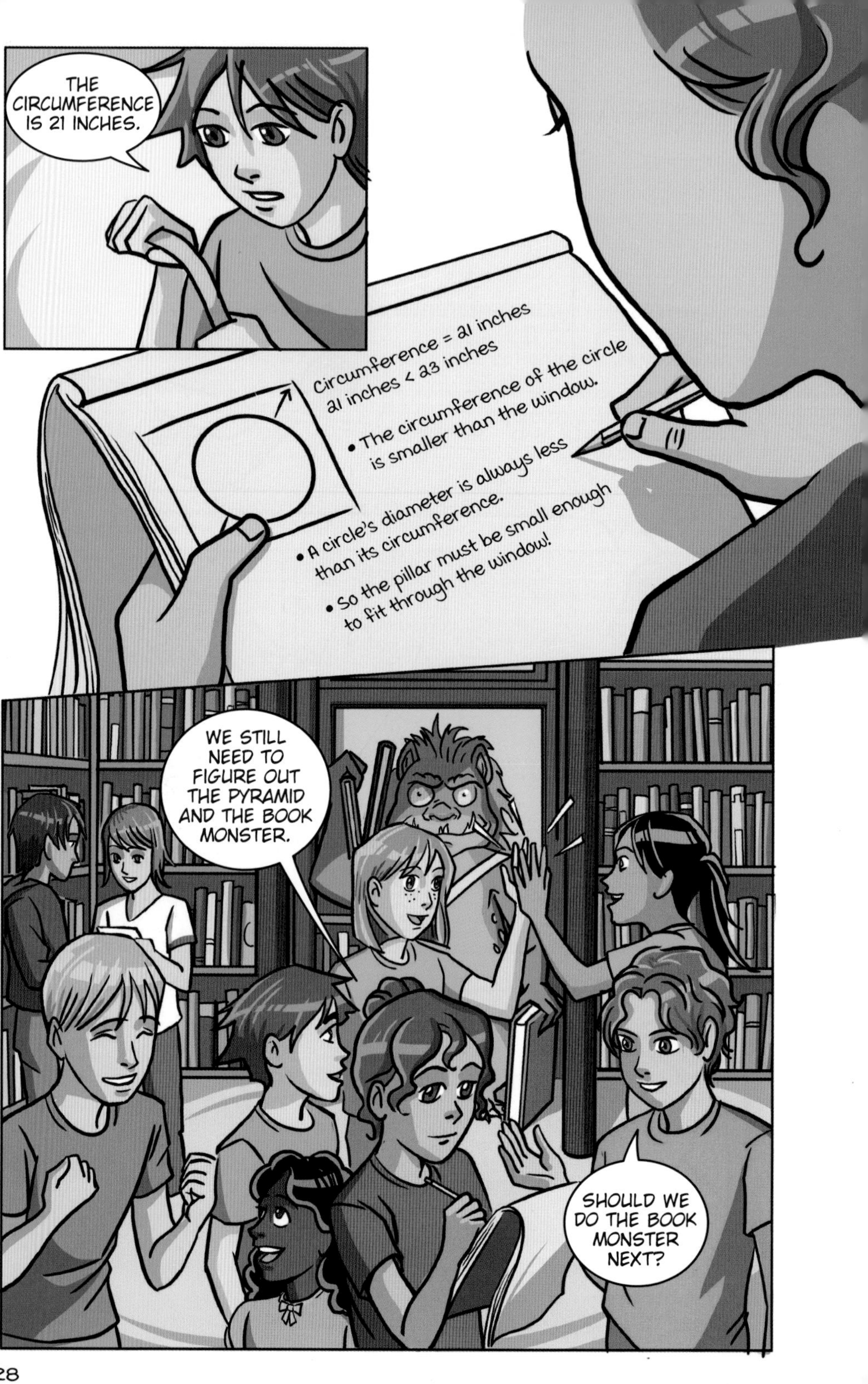
THE CIRCUMFERENCE IS 21 INCHES.
Circumference = 21 inches
21 inches < 23 inches
• The circumference of the circle is smaller than the window.
• A circle's diameter is always less than its circumference.
• So the pillar must be small enough to fit through the window!
WE STILL NEED TO FIGURE OUT THE PYRAMID AND THE BOOK MONSTER.
SHOULD WE DO THE BOOK MONSTER NEXT?

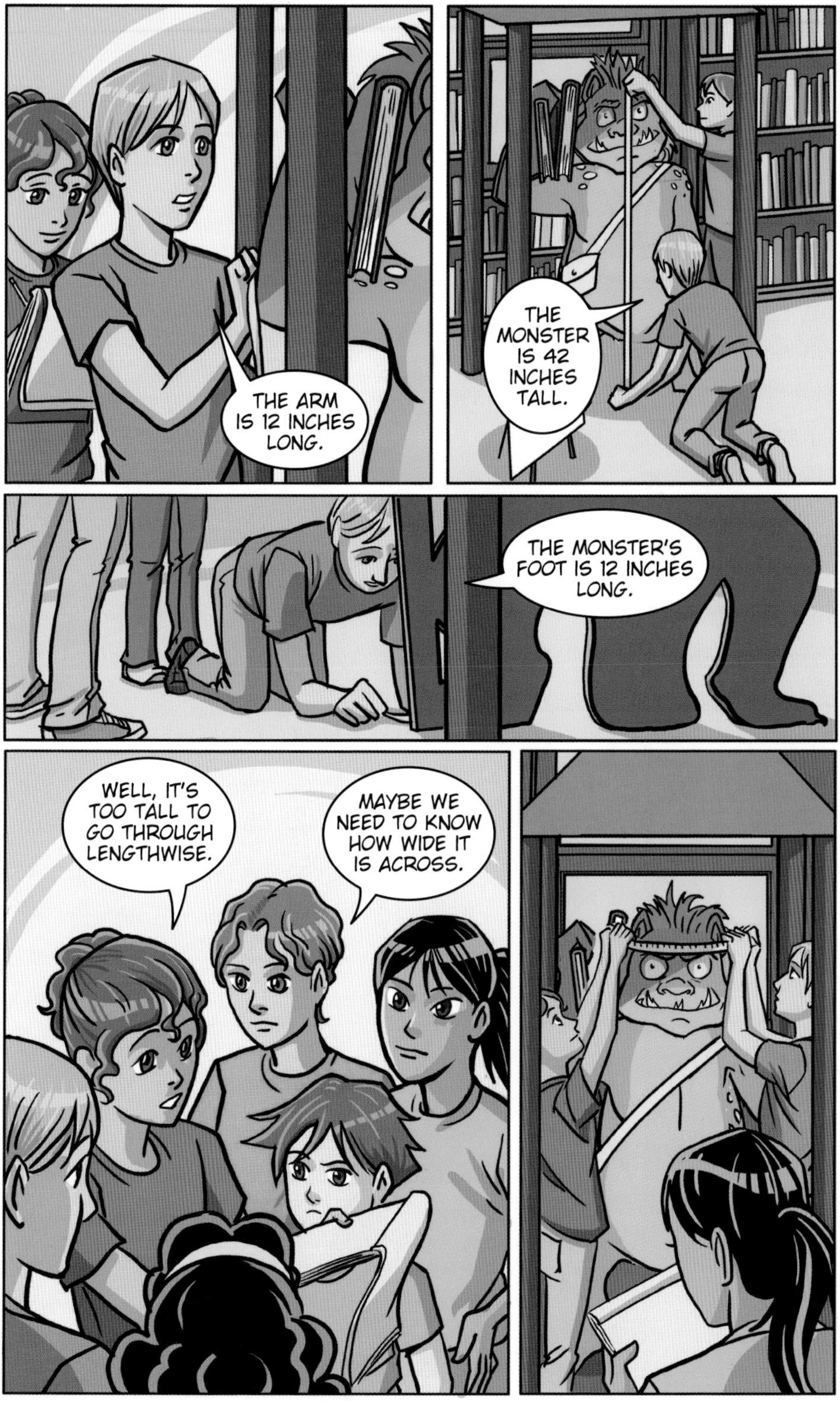
THE ARM IS 12 INCHES LONG.
THE MONSTER IS 42 INCHES TALL.
THE MONSTER'S FOOT IS 12 INCHES LONG.
WELL, IT'S TOO TALL TO GO THROUGH LENGTHWISE.
MAYBE WE NEED TO KNOW HOW WIDE IT IS ACROSS.

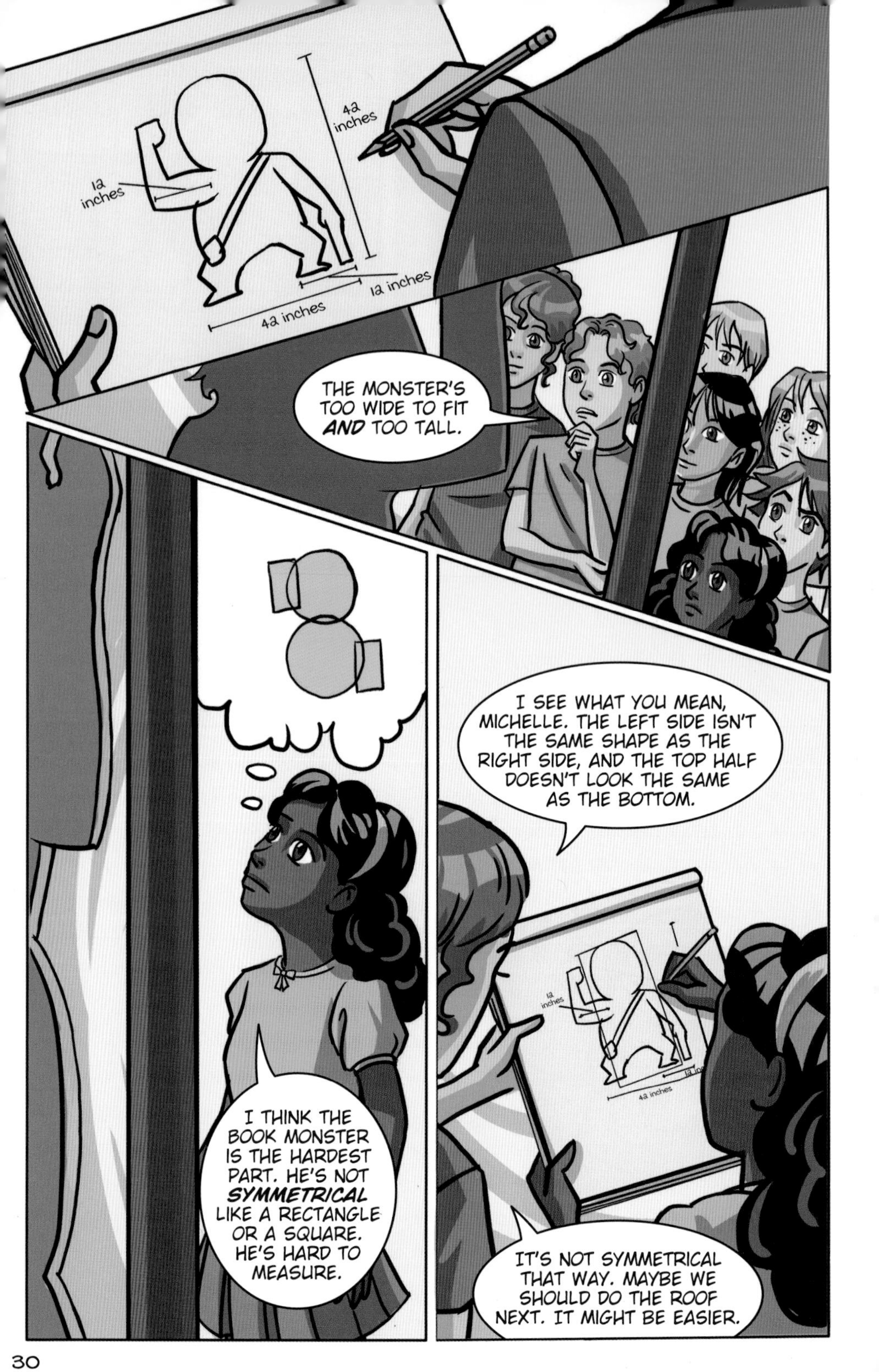

4a inches
12 inches
12 inches
4a inches
THE MONSTER'S TOO WIDE TO FIT **AND** TOO TALL.
I THINK THE BOOK MONSTER IS THE HARDEST PART. HE'S NOT ***SYMMETRICAL*** LIKE A RECTANGLE OR A SQUARE. HE'S HARD TO MEASURE.
I SEE WHAT YOU MEAN, MICHELLE. THE LEFT SIDE ISN'T THE SAME SHAPE AS THE RIGHT SIDE, AND THE TOP HALF DOESN'T LOOK THE SAME AS THE BOTTOM.
IT'S NOT SYMMETRICAL THAT WAY. MAYBE WE SHOULD DO THE ROOF NEXT. IT MIGHT BE EASIER.

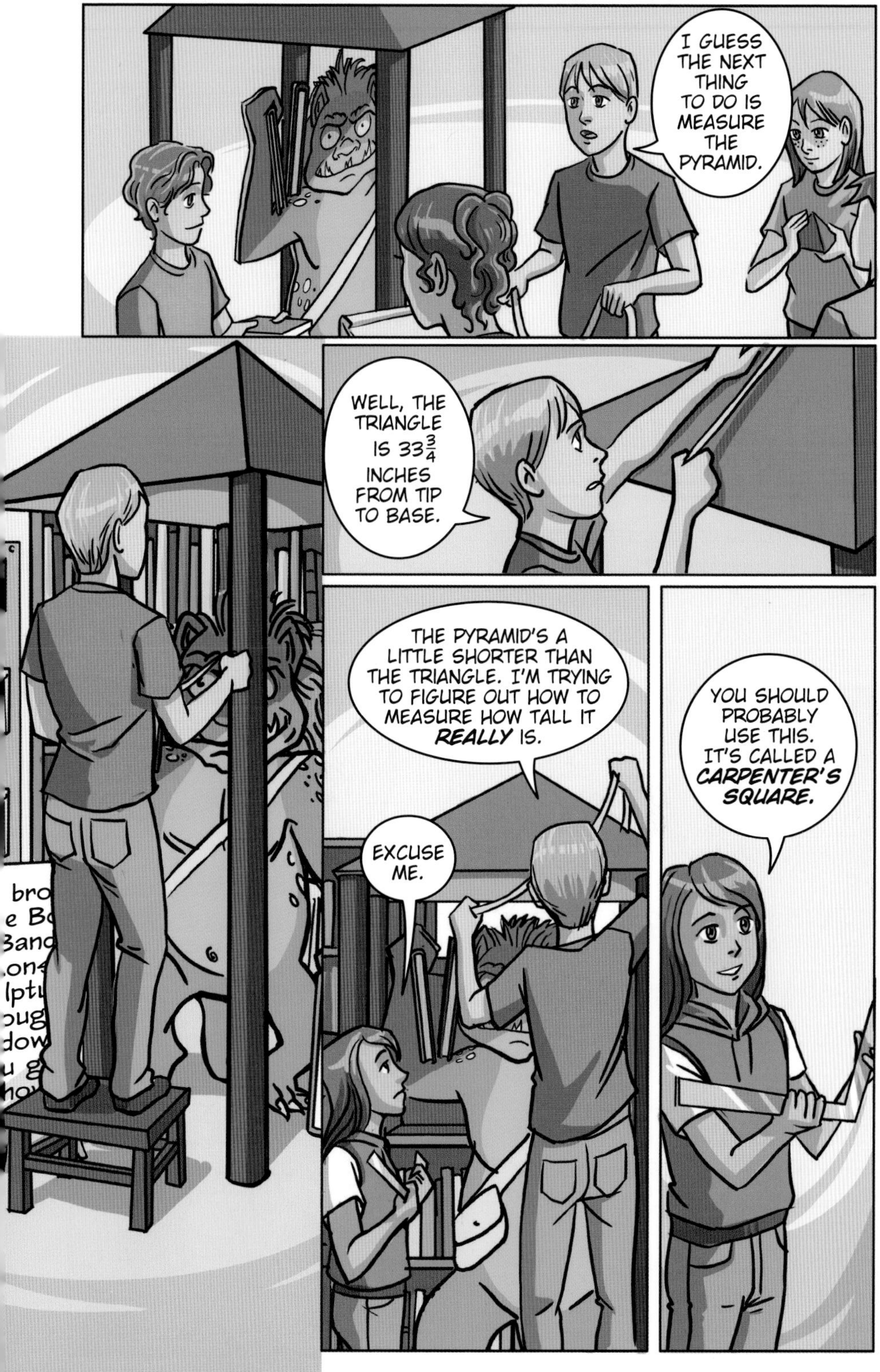
I GUESS THE NEXT THING TO DO IS MEASURE THE PYRAMID.
WELL, THE TRIANGLE IS $33\frac{3}{4}$ INCHES FROM TIP TO BASE.
THE PYRAMID'S A LITTLE SHORTER THAN THE TRIANGLE. I'M TRYING TO FIGURE OUT HOW TO MEASURE HOW TALL IT ***REALLY*** IS.
EXCUSE ME.
YOU SHOULD PROBABLY USE THIS. IT'S CALLED A ***CARPENTER'S SQUARE.***

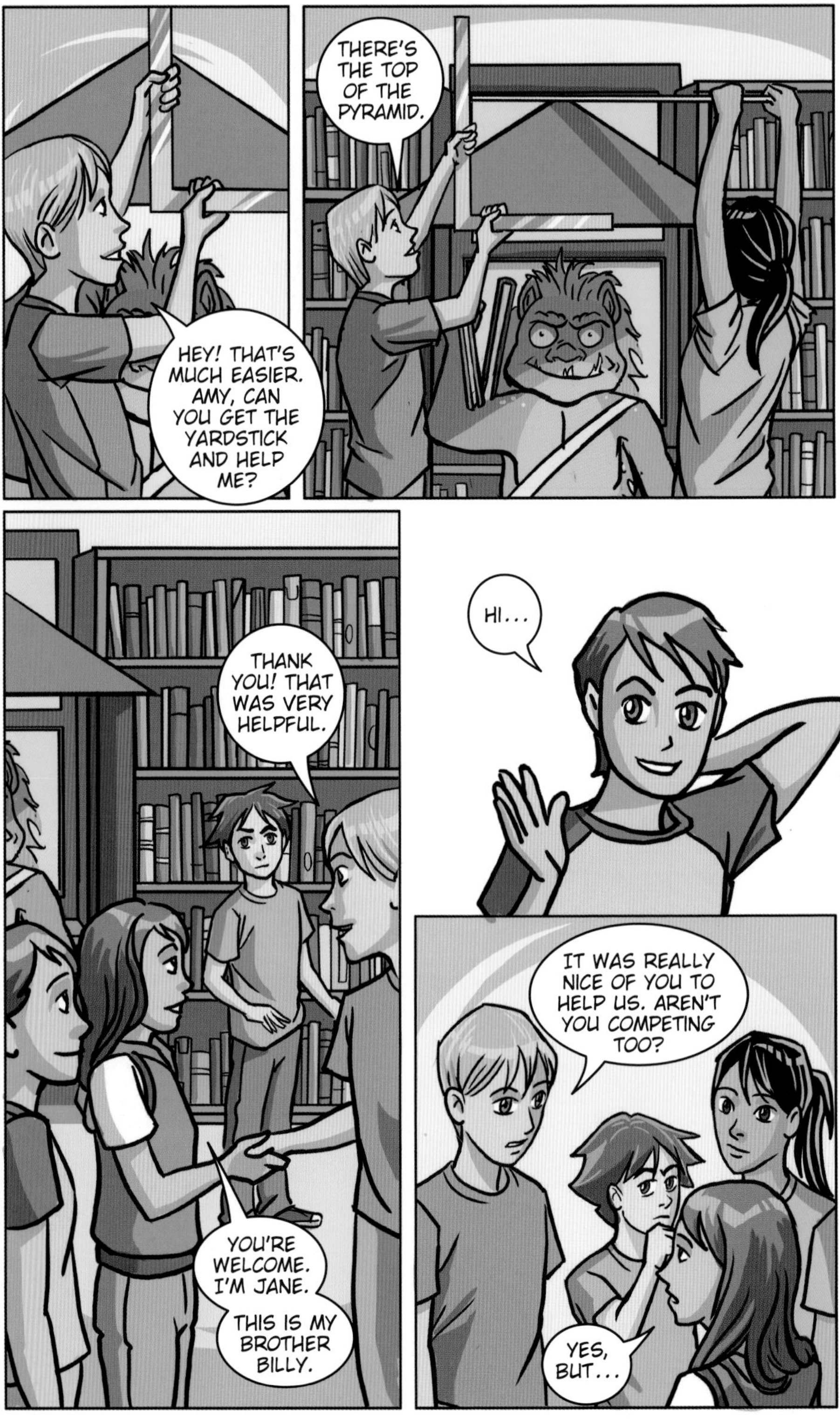
HEY! THAT'S MUCH EASIER. AMY, CAN YOU GET THE YARDSTICK AND HELP ME?
THERE'S THE TOP OF THE PYRAMID.
THANK YOU! THAT WAS VERY HELPFUL.
YOU'RE WELCOME. I'M JANE.
THIS IS MY BROTHER BILLY.
HI...
IT WAS REALLY NICE OF YOU TO HELP US. AREN'T YOU COMPETING TOO?
YES, BUT...

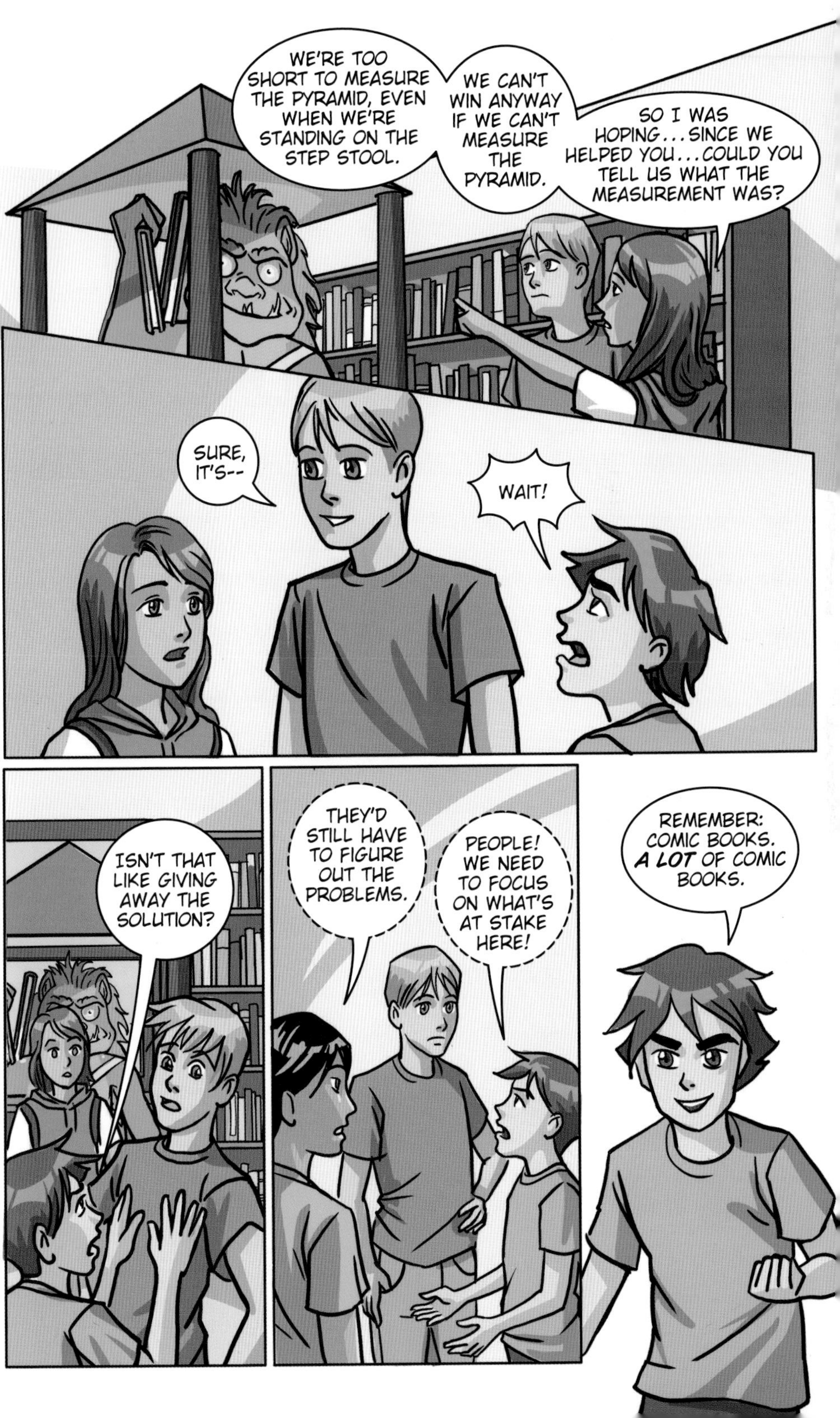
WE'RE TOO SHORT TO MEASURE THE PYRAMID, EVEN WHEN WE'RE STANDING ON THE STEP STOOL.
WE CAN'T WIN ANYWAY IF WE CAN'T MEASURE THE PYRAMID.
SO I WAS HOPING... SINCE WE HELPED YOU... COULD YOU TELL US WHAT THE MEASUREMENT WAS?
SURE, IT'S--
WAIT!
ISN'T THAT LIKE GIVING AWAY THE SOLUTION?
THEY'D STILL HAVE TO FIGURE OUT THE PROBLEMS.
PEOPLE! WE NEED TO FOCUS ON WHAT'S AT STAKE HERE!
REMEMBER: COMIC BOOKS. ***A LOT*** OF COMIC BOOKS.

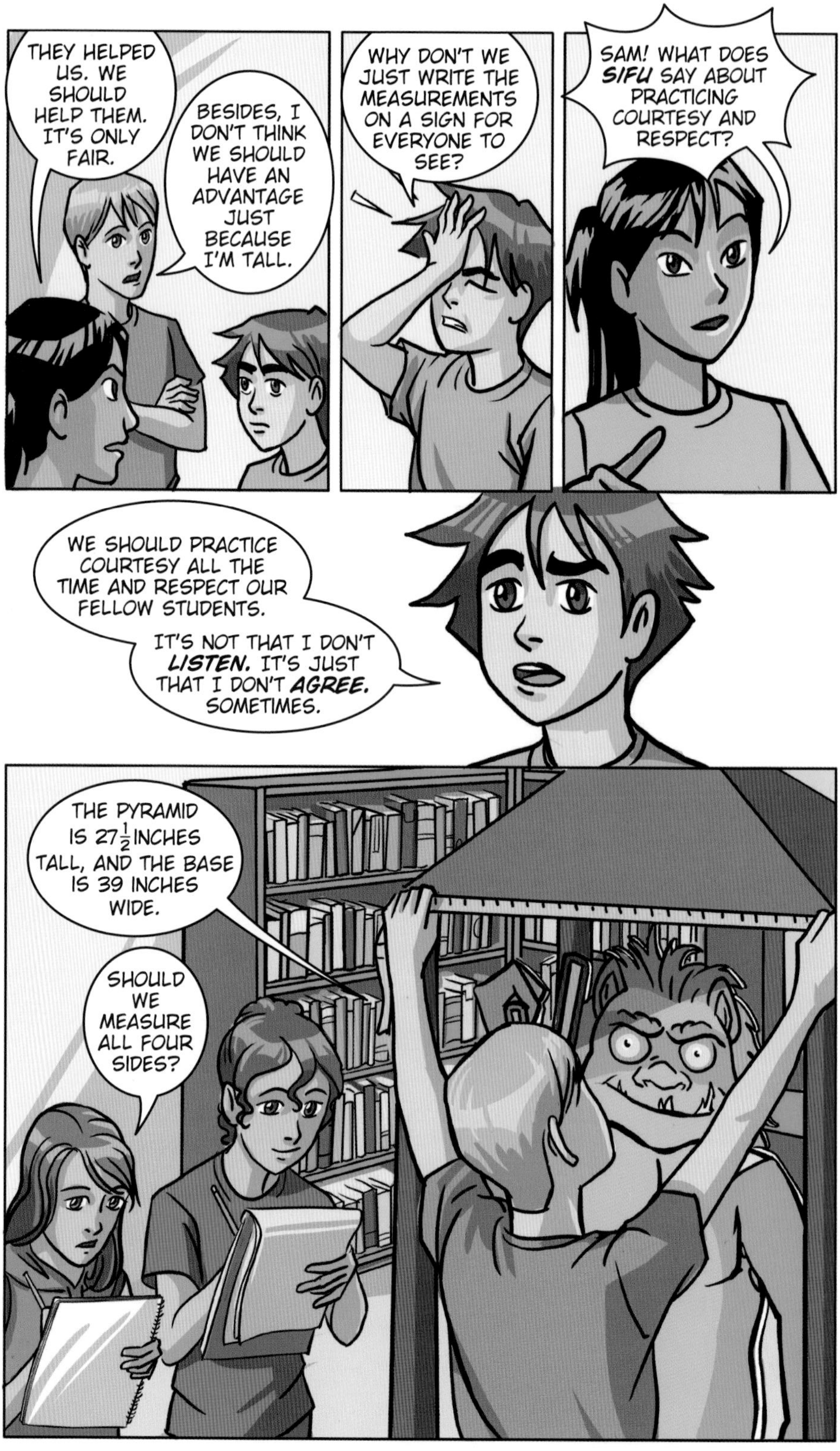
THEY HELPED US. WE SHOULD HELP THEM. IT'S ONLY FAIR.
BESIDES, I DON'T THINK WE SHOULD HAVE AN ADVANTAGE JUST BECAUSE I'M TALL.
WHY DON'T WE JUST WRITE THE MEASUREMENTS ON A SIGN FOR EVERYONE TO SEE?
SAM! WHAT DOES *SIFU* SAY ABOUT PRACTICING COURTESY AND RESPECT?
WE SHOULD PRACTICE COURTESY ALL THE TIME AND RESPECT OUR FELLOW STUDENTS.
IT'S NOT THAT I DON'T ***LISTEN.*** IT'S JUST THAT I DON'T ***AGREE.*** SOMETIMES.
THE PYRAMID IS 27½ INCHES TALL, AND THE BASE IS 39 INCHES WIDE.
SHOULD WE MEASURE ALL FOUR SIDES?

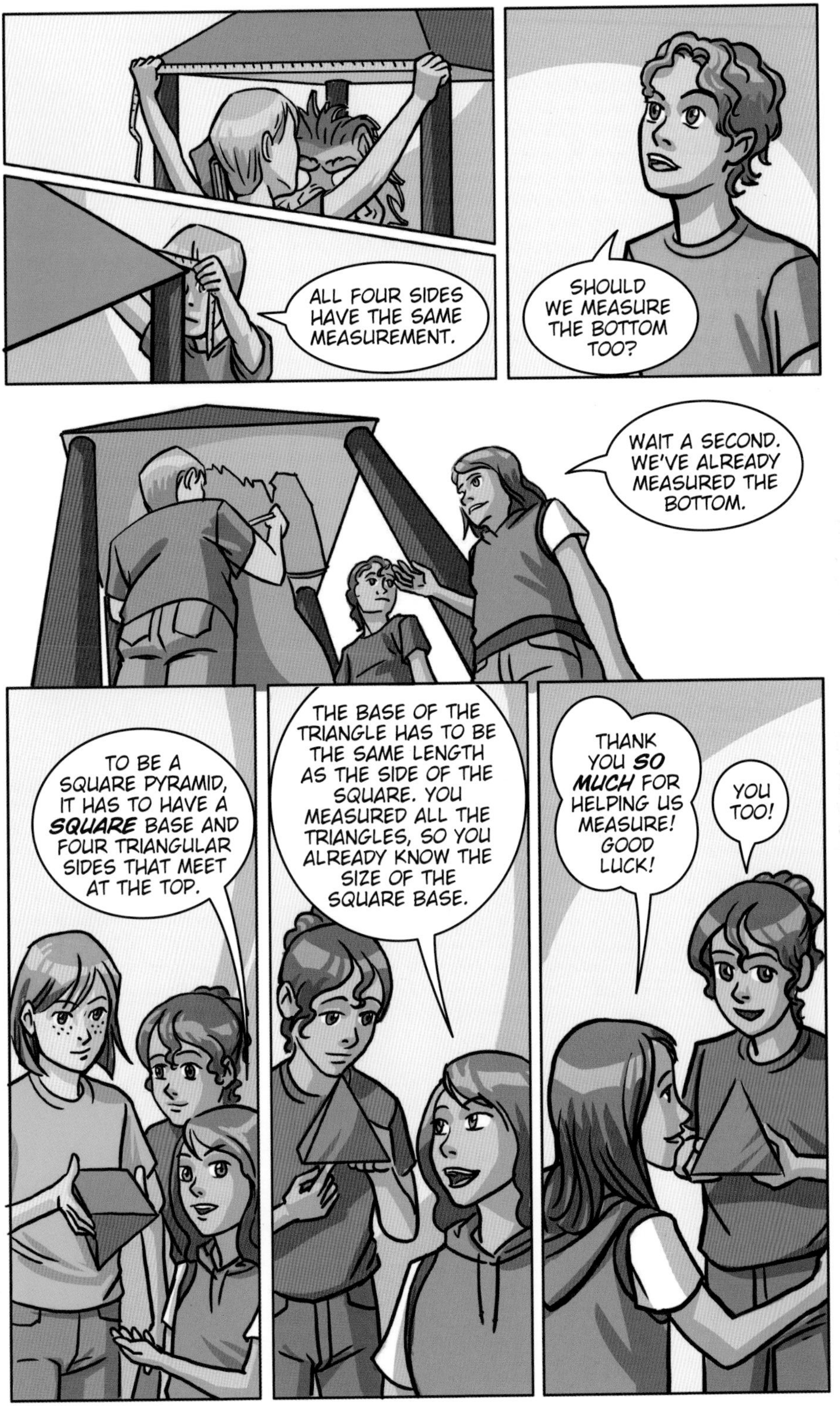
ALL FOUR SIDES HAVE THE SAME MEASUREMENT.
SHOULD WE MEASURE THE BOTTOM TOO?
WAIT A SECOND. WE'VE ALREADY MEASURED THE BOTTOM.
TO BE A SQUARE PYRAMID, IT HAS TO HAVE A ***SQUARE*** BASE AND FOUR TRIANGULAR SIDES THAT MEET AT THE TOP.
THE BASE OF THE TRIANGLE HAS TO BE THE SAME LENGTH AS THE SIDE OF THE SQUARE. YOU MEASURED ALL THE TRIANGLES, SO YOU ALREADY KNOW THE SIZE OF THE SQUARE BASE.
THANK YOU ***SO MUCH*** FOR HELPING US MEASURE! GOOD LUCK!
YOU TOO!

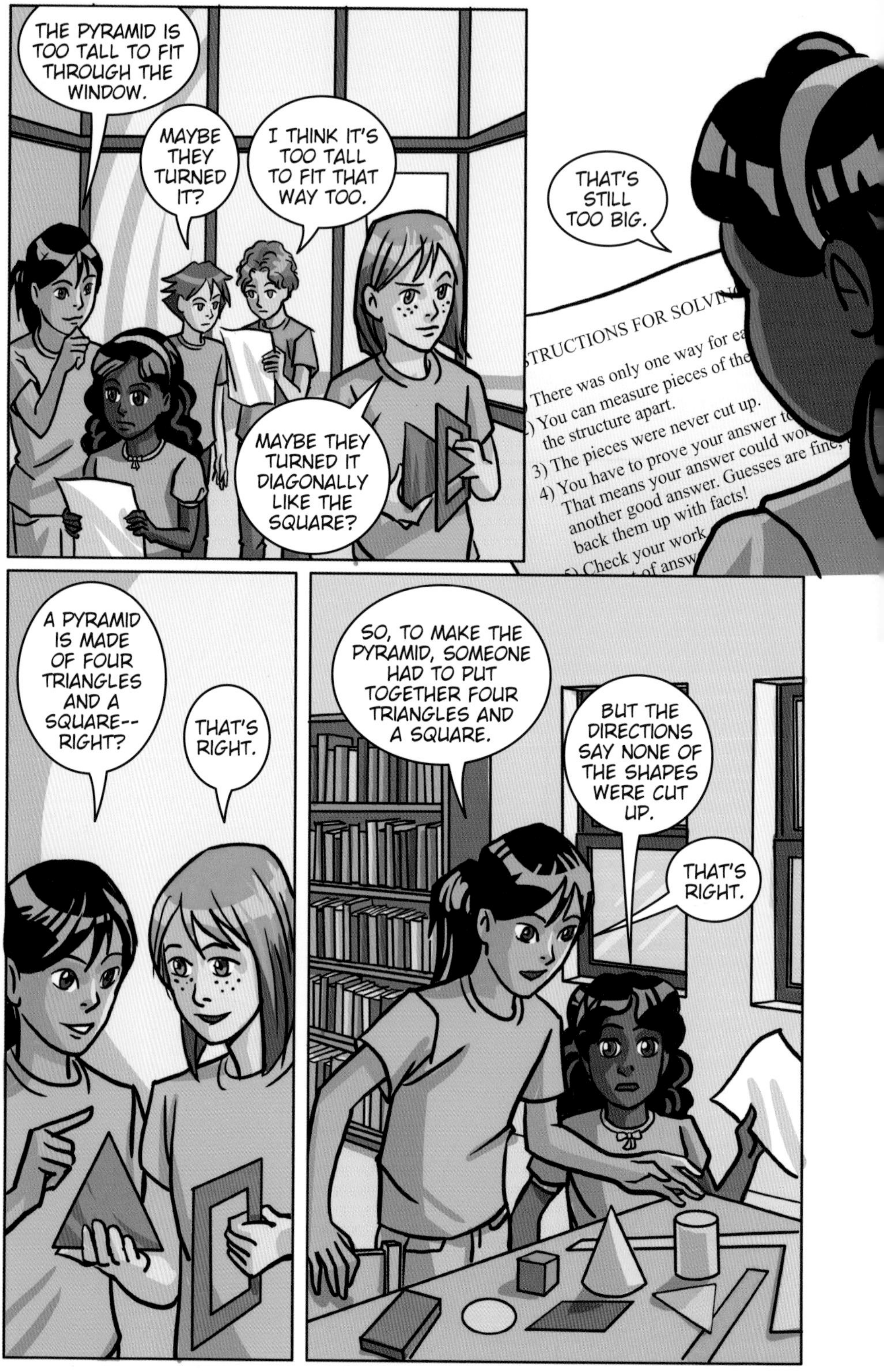
THE PYRAMID IS TOO TALL TO FIT THROUGH THE WINDOW.
MAYBE THEY TURNED IT?
I THINK IT'S TOO TALL TO FIT THAT WAY TOO.
MAYBE THEY TURNED IT DIAGONALLY LIKE THE SQUARE?
THAT'S STILL TOO BIG.
STRUCTIONS FOR SOLVIN
There was only one way for ea
) You can measure pieces of the
the structure apart.
3) The pieces were never cut up.
4) You have to prove your answer t
That means your answer could wo
another good answer. Guesses are fine
back them up with facts!
Check your work
A PYRAMID IS MADE OF FOUR TRIANGLES AND A SQUARE--RIGHT?
THAT'S RIGHT.
SO, TO MAKE THE PYRAMID, SOMEONE HAD TO PUT TOGETHER FOUR TRIANGLES AND A SQUARE.
BUT THE DIRECTIONS SAY NONE OF THE SHAPES WERE CUT UP.
THAT'S RIGHT.

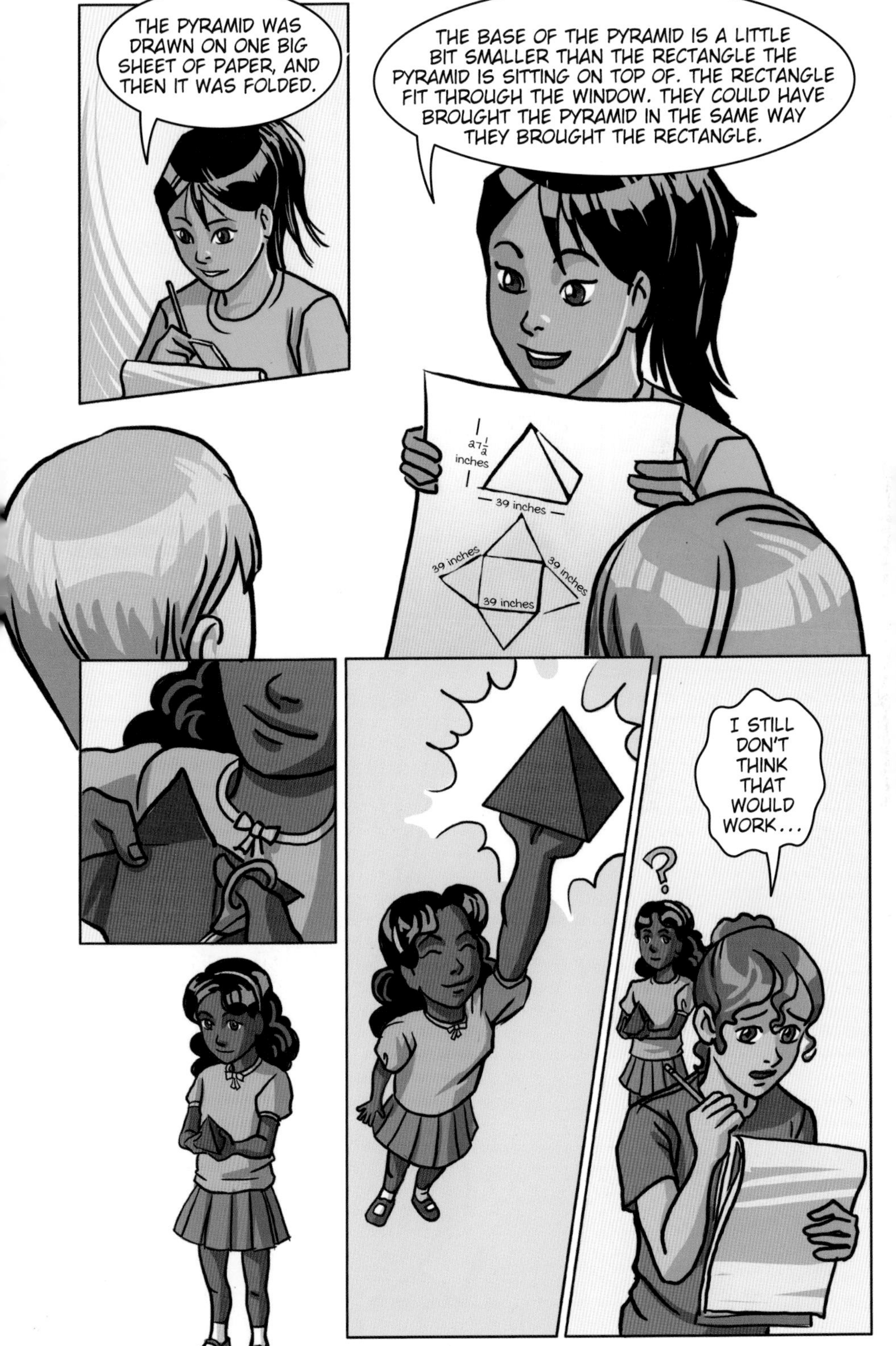
THE PYRAMID WAS DRAWN ON ONE BIG SHEET OF PAPER, AND THEN IT WAS FOLDED.
THE BASE OF THE PYRAMID IS A LITTLE BIT SMALLER THAN THE RECTANGLE THE PYRAMID IS SITTING ON TOP OF. THE RECTANGLE FIT THROUGH THE WINDOW. THEY COULD HAVE BROUGHT THE PYRAMID IN THE SAME WAY THEY BROUGHT THE RECTANGLE.
27 1/2 inches
39 inches
39 inches
39 inches
39 inches
I STILL DON'T THINK THAT WOULD WORK...

THE SQUARE BASE OF THE PYRAMID IS BARELY SMALL ENOUGH TO FIT THROUGH THE WINDOW. ADDING TRIANGLES TO EACH SIDES OF THE SQUARE WOULD DEFINITELY MAKE IT TOO BIG.

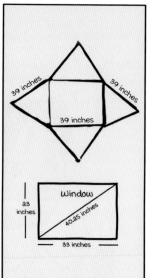

39 inches

39 inches

39 inches

23 inches

Window

40.25 inches

33 inches

YOU'RE RIGHT, JOY. THE PIECES ARE WAY TOO BIG TO FIT THAT WAY.

MAYBE THEY FOLDED... HMM...

WHAT ARE YOU THINKING, MICHELLE?

MAYBE THEY FOLDED THE PIECE ONE WAY TO GET IT THROUGH THE WINDOW AND THEN FOLDED IT A DIFFERENT WAY TO MAKE THE PYRAMID.

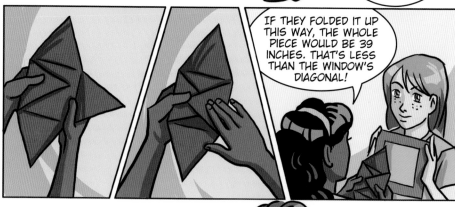

IF THEY FOLDED IT UP THIS WAY, THE WHOLE PIECE WOULD BE 39 INCHES. THAT'S LESS THAN THE WINDOW'S DIAGONAL!

THE PYRAMID IS MADE OF ONE PIECE THAT'S BEEN FOLDED.

THE PERSON FOLDED TWO OF THE TRIANGLES FLAT TO GET THE PIECE THROUGH THE WINDOW.

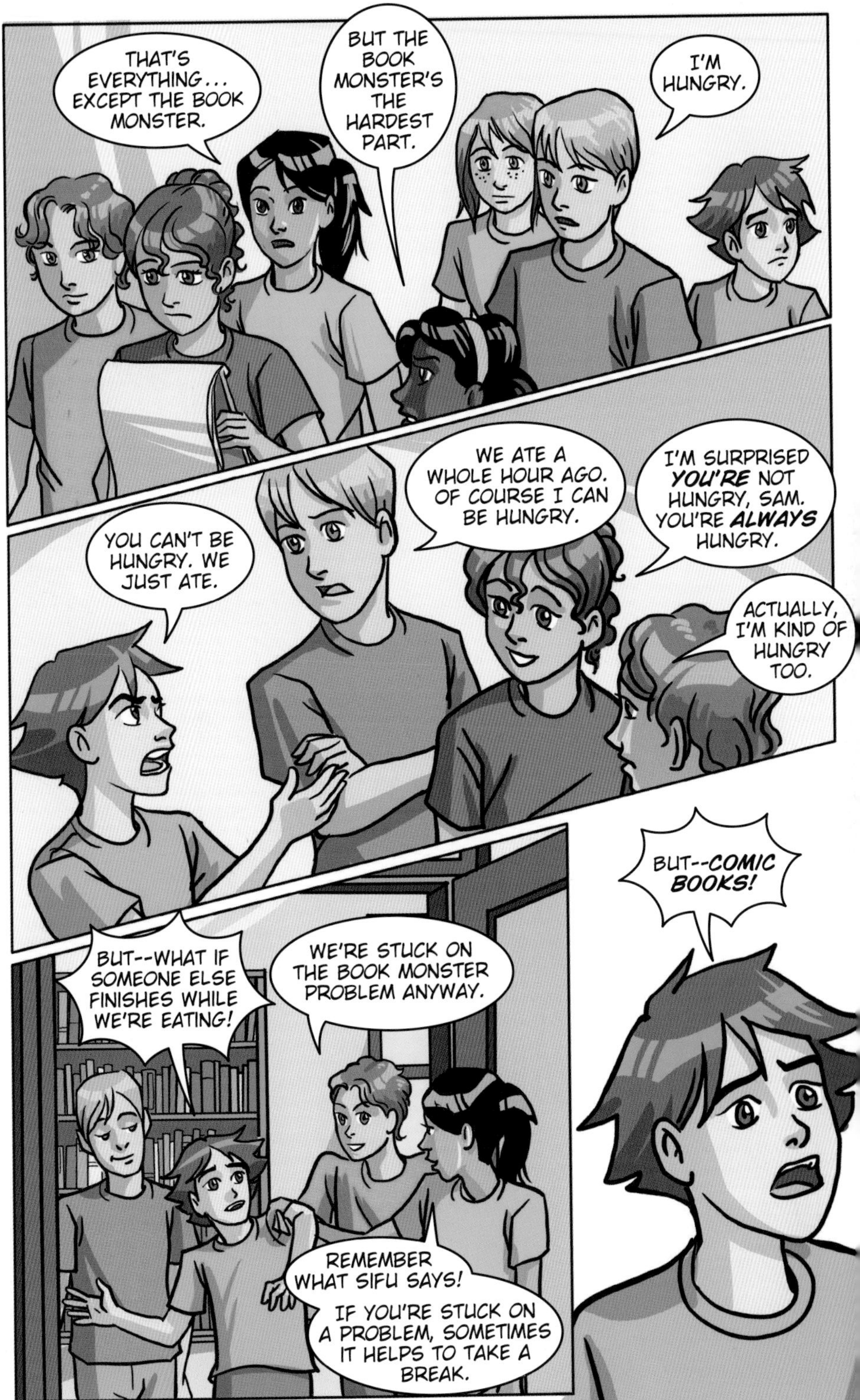
THAT'S EVERYTHING... EXCEPT THE BOOK MONSTER.
BUT THE BOOK MONSTER'S THE HARDEST PART.
I'M HUNGRY.
YOU CAN'T BE HUNGRY. WE JUST ATE.
WE ATE A WHOLE HOUR AGO. OF COURSE I CAN BE HUNGRY.
I'M SURPRISED ***YOU'RE*** NOT HUNGRY, SAM. YOU'RE ***ALWAYS*** HUNGRY.
ACTUALLY, I'M KIND OF HUNGRY TOO.
BUT--WHAT IF SOMEONE ELSE FINISHES WHILE WE'RE EATING!
WE'RE STUCK ON THE BOOK MONSTER PROBLEM ANYWAY.
REMEMBER WHAT SIFU SAYS!
IF YOU'RE STUCK ON A PROBLEM, SOMETIMES IT HELPS TO TAKE A BREAK.
BUT--***COMIC BOOKS!***

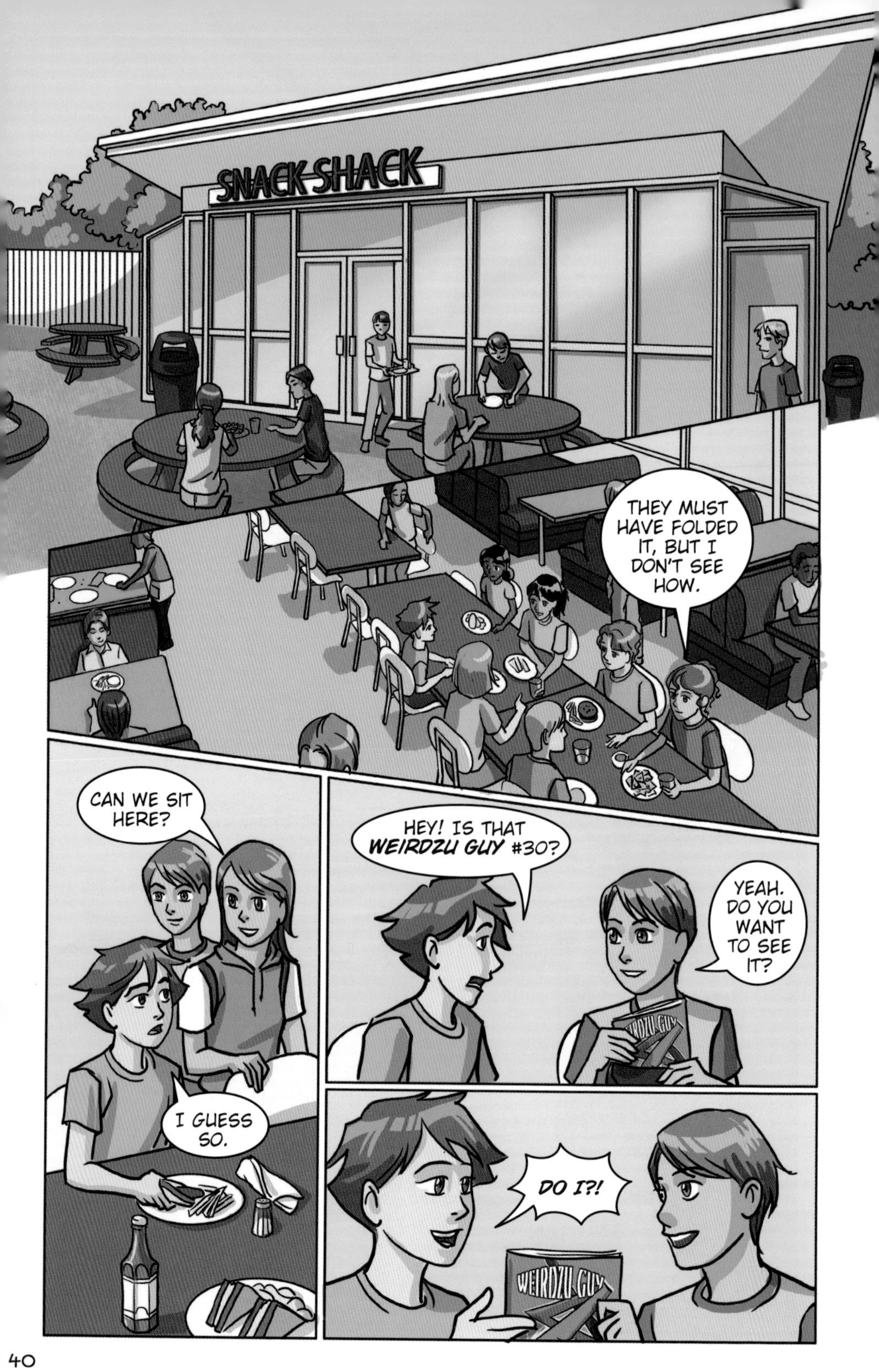
SNACK SHACK
THEY MUST HAVE FOLDED IT, BUT I DON'T SEE HOW.
CAN WE SIT HERE?
I GUESS SO.
HEY! IS THAT *WEIRDZU GUY* #30?
YEAH. DO YOU WANT TO SEE IT?
WEIRDZU GUY
DO I?!
WEIRDZU GUY

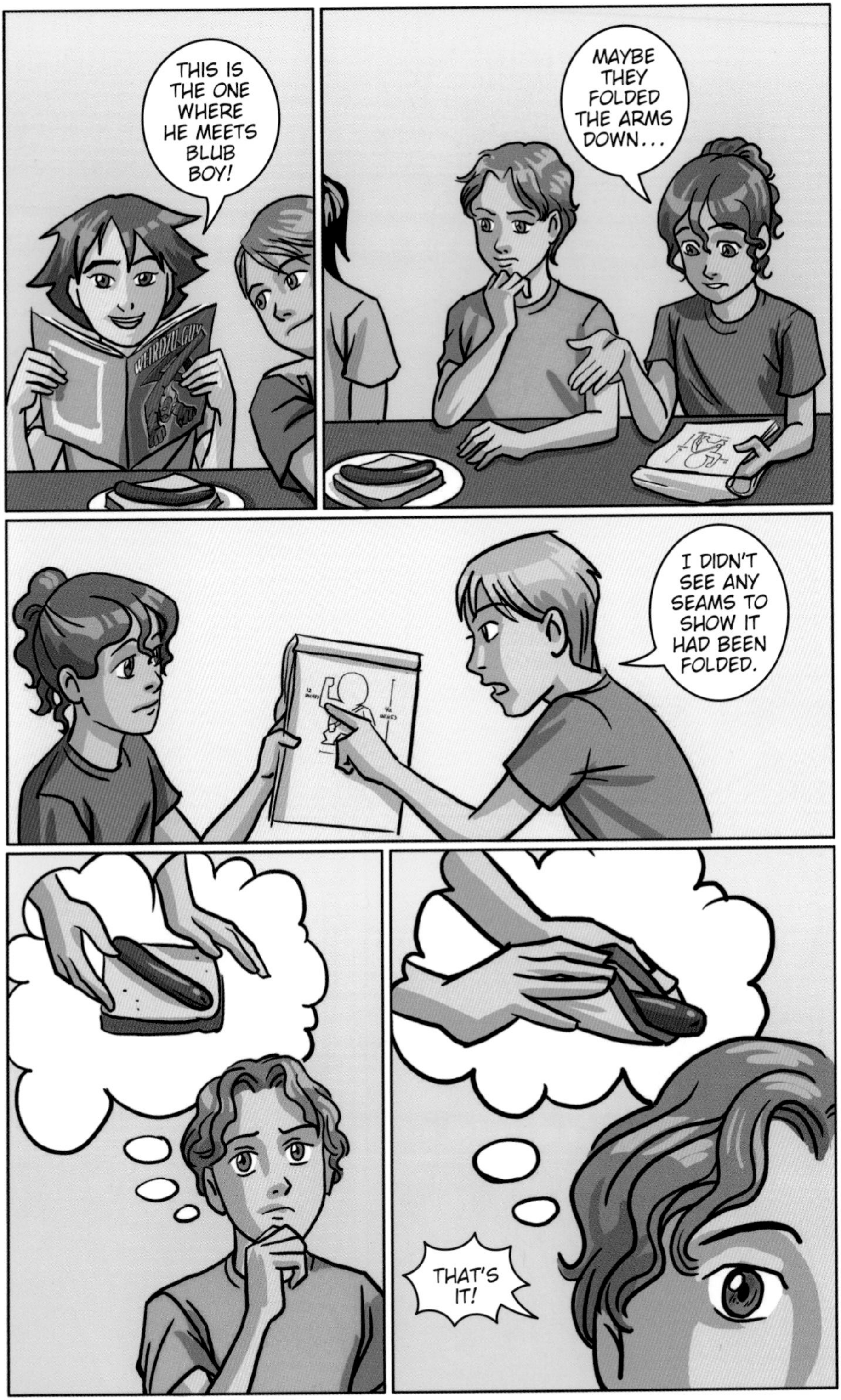
THIS IS THE ONE WHERE HE MEETS BLUB BOY!
MAYBE THEY FOLDED THE ARMS DOWN...
I DIDN'T SEE ANY SEAMS TO SHOW IT HAD BEEN FOLDED.
THAT'S IT!

MICHELLE SAID THE BOOK MONSTER ISN'T SYMMETRICAL, BUT THAT WASN'T REALLY TRUE.

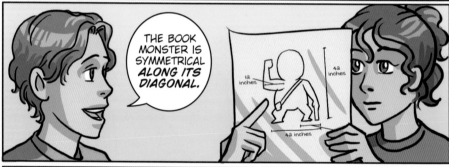

THE BOOK MONSTER IS SYMMETRICAL *ALONG ITS DIAGONAL.*

12 inches

42 inches

42 inches

I BET THE SCIENCE STARS FOLDED THE BOOK MONSTER ALONG ITS DIAGONAL. WE SHOULD MEASURE TO SEE IF IT WOULD FIT THAT WAY.

THAT'S A GREAT IDEA!

THANKS FOR LETTING ME LOOK AT YOUR COMIC BOOK!

SURE!

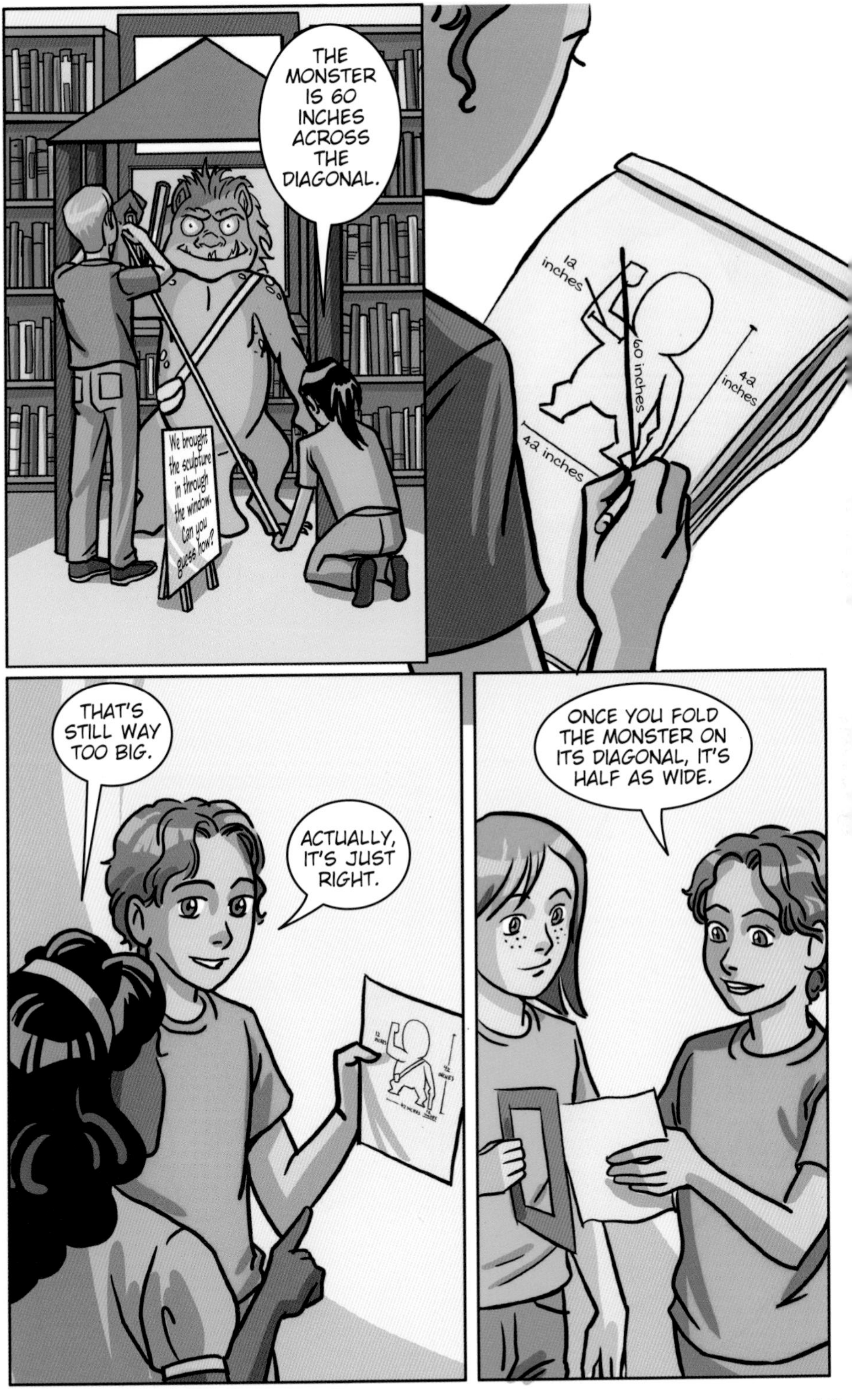

THE MONSTER IS 60 INCHES ACROSS THE DIAGONAL.
We brought the sculpture in through the window. Can you guess how?
12 inches
60 inches
42 inches
42 inches
THAT'S STILL WAY TOO BIG.
ACTUALLY, IT'S JUST RIGHT.
ONCE YOU FOLD THE MONSTER ON ITS DIAGONAL, IT'S HALF AS WIDE.

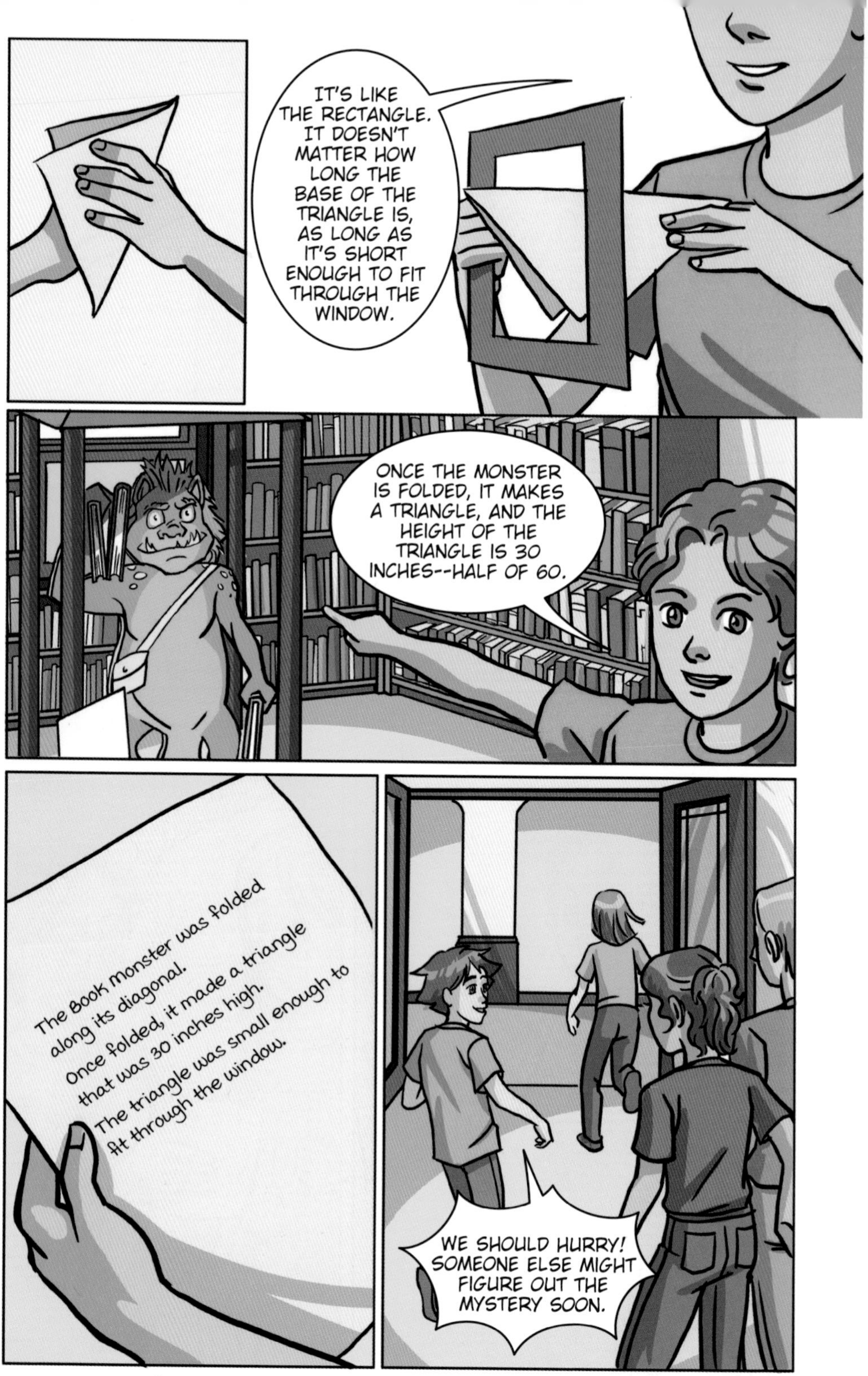
IT'S LIKE THE RECTANGLE. IT DOESN'T MATTER HOW LONG THE BASE OF THE TRIANGLE IS, AS LONG AS IT'S SHORT ENOUGH TO FIT THROUGH THE WINDOW.
ONCE THE MONSTER IS FOLDED, IT MAKES A TRIANGLE, AND THE HEIGHT OF THE TRIANGLE IS 30 INCHES--HALF OF 60.
The Book monster was folded along its diagonal. Once folded, it made a triangle that was 30 inches high. The triangle was small enough to fit through the window.
WE SHOULD HURRY! SOMEONE ELSE MIGHT FIGURE OUT THE MYSTERY SOON.

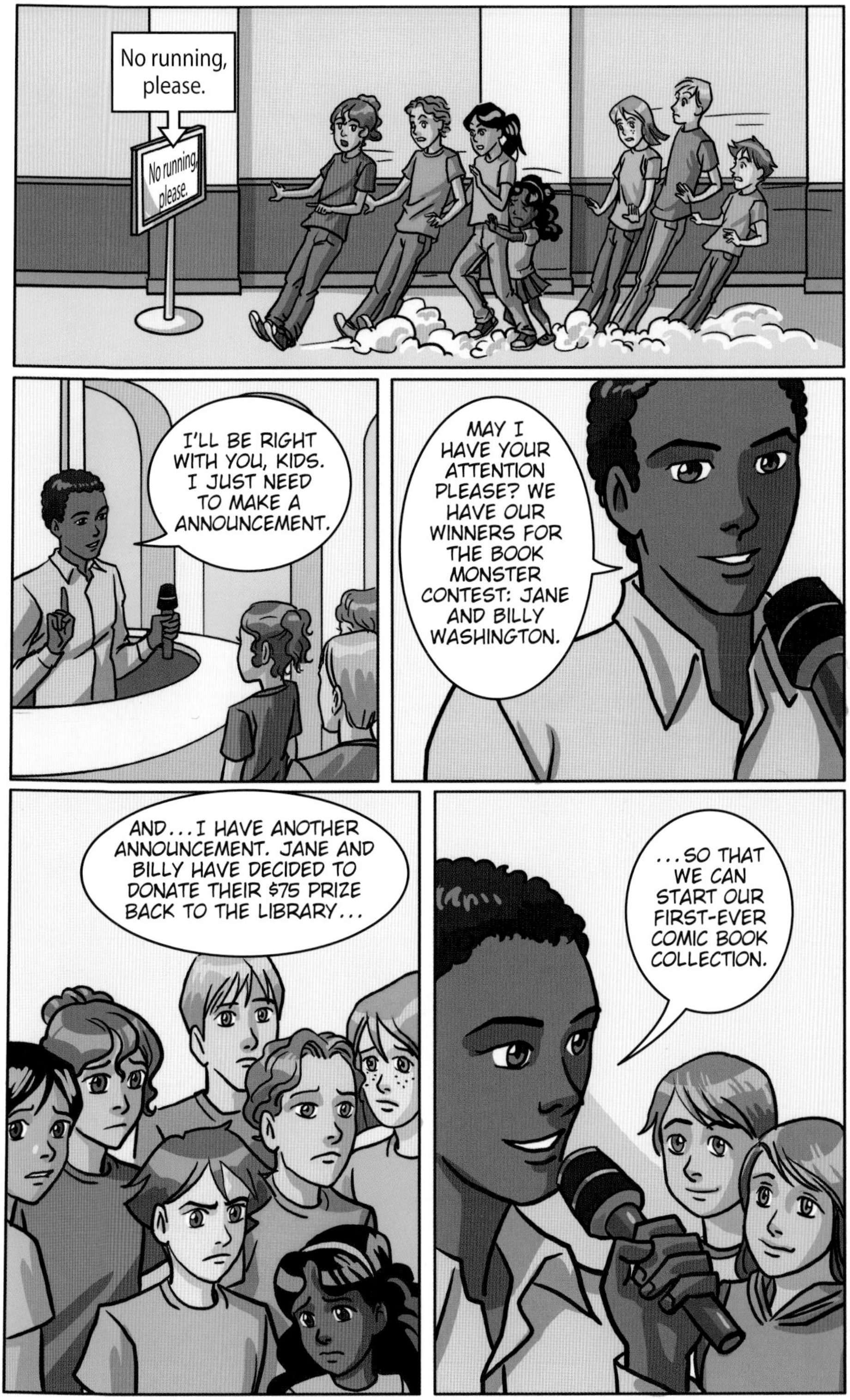
No running, please.
No running, please.
I'LL BE RIGHT WITH YOU, KIDS. I JUST NEED TO MAKE A ANNOUNCEMENT.
MAY I HAVE YOUR ATTENTION PLEASE? WE HAVE OUR WINNERS FOR THE BOOK MONSTER CONTEST: JANE AND BILLY WASHINGTON.
AND... I HAVE ANOTHER ANNOUNCEMENT. JANE AND BILLY HAVE DECIDED TO DONATE THEIR $75 PRIZE BACK TO THE LIBRARY...
...SO THAT WE CAN START OUR FIRST-EVER COMIC BOOK COLLECTION.

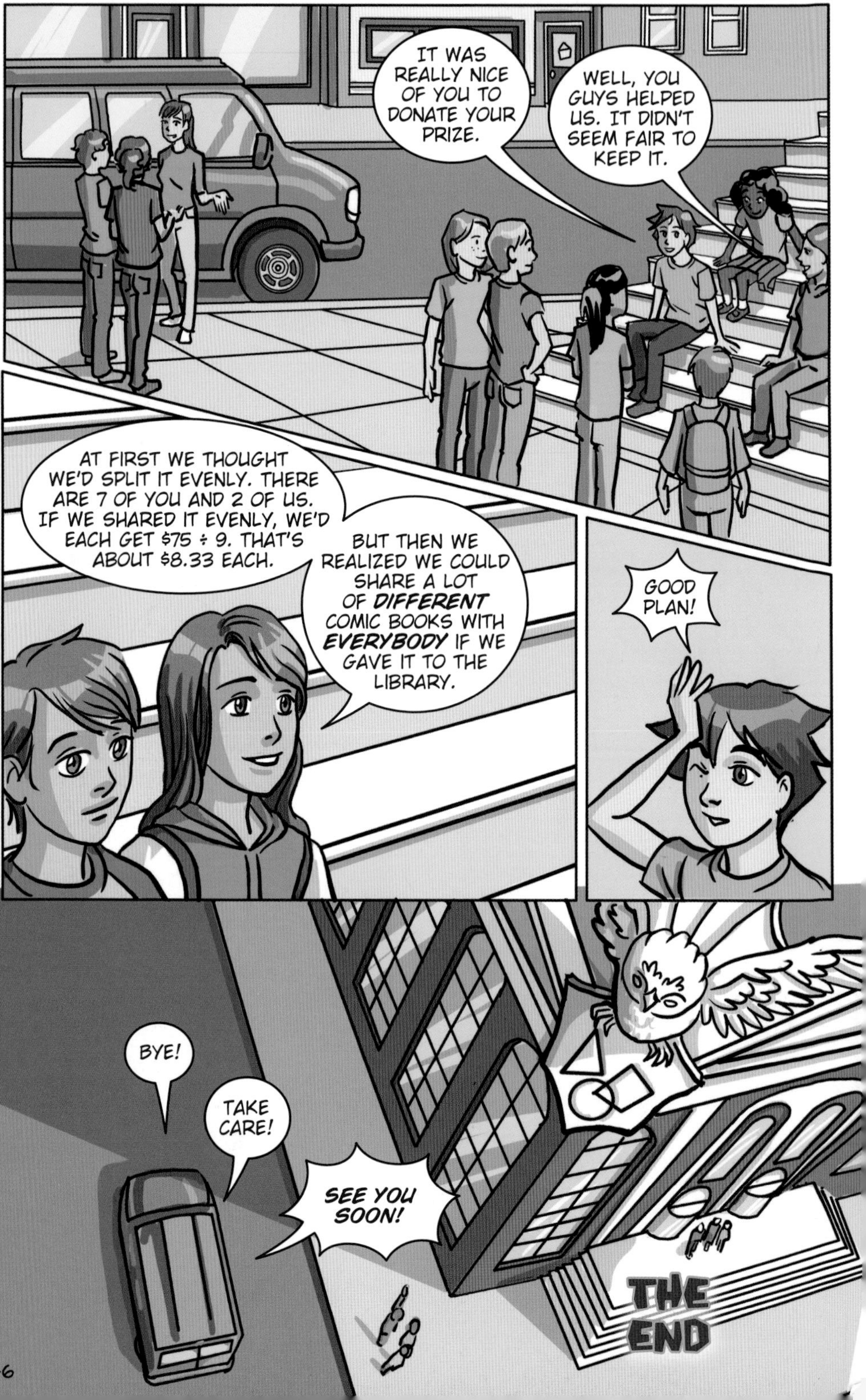
IT WAS REALLY NICE OF YOU TO DONATE YOUR PRIZE.
WELL, YOU GUYS HELPED US. IT DIDN'T SEEM FAIR TO KEEP IT.
AT FIRST WE THOUGHT WE'D SPLIT IT EVENLY. THERE ARE 7 OF YOU AND 2 OF US. IF WE SHARED IT EVENLY, WE'D EACH GET $75 ÷ 9. THAT'S ABOUT $8.33 EACH.
BUT THEN WE REALIZED WE COULD SHARE A LOT OF ***DIFFERENT*** COMIC BOOKS WITH ***EVERYBODY*** IF WE GAVE IT TO THE LIBRARY.
GOOD PLAN!
BYE!
TAKE CARE!
SEE YOU SOON!
THE END

The Author

Melinda Thielbar is a teacher who has written math courses for all ages, from kids to adults. In 2005 Melinda was awarded a VIGRE fellowship at North Carolina State University for PhD candidates "likely to make a strong contribution to education in mathematics." She lives in Raleigh, North Carolina, with her husband, author and video game programmer Richard Dansky, and their two cats.

Lydia Barriman is a is a teacher, doctoral candidate, and writer of math courses for all ages.

The Artists

Tintin Pantoja was born in Manila in the Philippines. She received a degree in Illustration and Cartooning from the School of Visual Arts (SVA) in New York City and was nominated for the Friends of Lulu "Best Newcomer" award. She was also a finalist in Tokyopop's Rising Stars of Manga 5.

Yali Lin was born in southern China and lived there for 11 years before moving to New York and graduating from SVA. She loves climbing trees, walking barefoot on grass, and chasing dragonflies. When not drawing, she teaches cartooning to teens.

Becky Grutzik received a degree in illustration from the University of Wisconsin-Stevens Point. In her free time, she and her husband, Matt Wendt, teach a class to kids on how to draw manga and superheroes.

Jenn Manley Lee was born in Clovis, New Mexico. After many travels, she settled in Portland, Oregon, where she works as a graphic designer. She keeps the home she shares with spouse Kip Manley and daughter Taran full of books, geeks, art, cats, and music.

Candice Chow studied animation at SVA and followed her interests through comics, manga, and graphic design. Her previous books include *Macbeth* (Wiley) with fellow SVA graduate **Eve Grandt**, who lives and works in Brooklyn, New York.

TOM BY JENN

MANGA MATH MYSTERIES #8

After the fence gate is left unlatched, Amy's playful new puppy, Brada, escapes! The other kids want to help Amy and her parents look for Brada. But to find her quickly, they will need to figure out where she's most likely to go. They'll use what they know about where she's gone in the past—and probability—to find . . .

THE RUNAWAY PUPPY

JOIN THE KIDS FROM THE KUNG FU SCHOOL IN SOLVING ALL THE MANGA MATH MYSTERIES!

ART BY TINTIN PANTOJA

MANGA MATH MYSTERIES